The Dorset Boy book 14 – Revolution

This is a work of Fiction. All characters and stories are fictional although based in historical settings. If you see your name appear in the story, it is a coincidence, or maybe I asked first.

Acknowledgements

Thanks to Dawn Spears the brilliant artist who created the cover artwork and my editor Debz Hobbs-Wyatt without whom the books wouldn't be as good as they are.

My wife who is so supportive and believes in me. Last my dogs Blaez and Zeeva and cats Vaskr and Rosa who watch me act out the fight scenes and must wonder what the hell has gotten into their boss. And a special thank you to Troy who was the grandfather of Blaez in real life. He was a magnificent beast just like his grandson!

THANK YOU FOR READING!

I hope you enjoy reading this book as much as I enjoyed writing it. Reviews are so helpful to authors. I really appreciate all reviews, both positive and negative. If you want to leave one, you can do so on Amazon, through my website, or on Twitter.

About the Author

Christopher C Tubbs is a dog-loving descendent of a long line of Dorset clay miners and has chased his family tree back to the 16th century in the Isle of Purbeck. He left school at sixteen to train as an Avionics Craftsman, has been a public speaker at conferences for most of his career and was one of the founders of a successful games company back in the 1990s. Now in his sixties, he finally writes the stories he had been dreaming about for years. Thanks to inspiration from great authors like Alexander Kent, Dewey Lambdin, Patrick O'Brian, Raymond E Feist, and Dudley Pope, he was finally able to put digit to keyboard. He lives in the Netherlands Antilles with his wife, two Dutch Shepherds, and two Norwegian Forest cats.

You can visit him on his website
www.thedorsetboy.com
The Dorset Boy, Facebook page.

Or tweet him @ChristopherCTu3

The Dorset Boy Series Timeline

1792 – 1795   Book 1: A Talent for Trouble
Marty joins the navy as an assistant steward and through a series of adventures ends up a midshipman.

1795 – 1798   Book 2: The Special Operations Flotilla
Marty is a founder member of the Special Operations Flotilla, learns to be a spy and passes as Lieutenant.

1799 – 1802   Book 3: Agent Provocateur
Marty teams up with Linette to infiltrate Paris, marries Caroline, becomes a father and fights pirates in Madagascar.

1802 – 1804   Book 4: In Dangerous Company
Marty and Caroline are in India helping out Arthur Wellesley, combatting French efforts to disrupt the East India Company and French-sponsored pirates on Reunion. James Stockley born.

1804 – 1805   Book 5: The Tempest
Piracy in the Caribbean, French interference, Spanish gold and the death of Nelson. Marty makes Captain.

1806 – 1807   Book 6: Vendetta
A favour carried out for a prince, a new ship, the S.O.F. move to Gibraltar, the battle of Maida, counter espionage in Malta and a Vendetta declared and closed.

1807 – 1809   Book 7: The Trojan Horse
Rescue of the Portuguese royal family, Battle of the Basque Roads with Thomas Cochrane, and back to the Indian Ocean and another conflict with the French Intelligence Service.

1809 – 1811   Book 8: La Licorne

Marty takes on the role of Viscount Wellington's Head of Intelligence. Battle of The Lines of Torres Vedras, siege of Cadiz, skulduggery, espionage and blowing stuff up to confound the French.

1812   Book 9: Raider

Marty is busy. From London to Paris to America and back to the Mediterranean for the battle of Salamanca. A mission to the Adriatic reveals a white-slavery racket that results in a private mission to the Caribbean to rescue his children.

1813 – 1814   Book 10: Silverthorn

Promoted to Commodore and given a viscountcy, Marty is sent to the Caribbean to be Governor of Aruba which provides the cover story he needs to fight American privateers and undermine the Spanish in South America. On his return he escorts Napoleon into Exile on Alba.

1815 – 1816   Book 11: Exile

After 100 days in exile Napoleon returns to France and Marty tries to hunt him down. After the battle of Waterloo Marty again escorts him into Exile on St Helena. His help is requested by the Governor of Ceylon against the rebels in Kandy.

1817 – 1818   Book 12: Dynasty

To Paris to stop an assassination, then the Mediterranean to further British interests in the region. Finally, to Calcutta as Military Attaché to take part in the war with the Maratha Empire. Beth comes into her own as a spy, but James prefers the navy life.

1818 -- 1819   Book 13: Empire
The end of the third Anglo-Maratha war and the establishment of the Raj. Intrigue in India, war with the Pindaris, the foundation of Singapore, shipwreck, sea wars and storms.

1820 - 1821   Book 14: Revolution
The Ottoman Empire is starting to disintegrate. The Greeks are starting to revolt. Marty has a promise to keep so Britain can gain Cyprus. Just to complicate things King John of Portugal needs his support as well.

Contents

Chapter 1: Arrival

The squadron returned to England in a sombre mood. Commodore Martin Stockley had informed them that they would be absorbed into the navy proper as the squadron was being disbanded on their return to Portsmouth. It was early in the year of our Lord 1820 and the weather reflected their mood.

They were passing the Isles of Scilly when the lookout called, "Deck there! The flags be flying at 'alf mast on that island!"

"That's odd. Give me a telescope," Marty said. He ran up the ratlines to the futtock shrouds then up to the topsail yard. Even at forty he was fit and was hardly breathing heavily when he got there. They were passing St Agnes and he could see the old town on St Mary's. There, very clearly, above St Mary's church the union flag flew at half-mast. He returned to the deck.

"Have the squadron heave to and instruct the Endellion to go into harbour and get the latest news," he said to Wolfgang.

Signals flew, were acknowledged, and the Unicorn came to a stop. Gently rocking on the slight sea. The Endellion, being a Cornish ship by origin, slipped into Old Town harbour flying the Cornish flag under the union flag. They were only there for a few minutes before beating back out and coming alongside the Unicorn. Philip Trenchard came aboard looking grim.

Marty, who wanted to hear what he had to say before the men, took him down into his cabin.

"Well, Richard, what's the bad news?"

"King George is dead. He died in January." He handed over a newspaper. It was *The Times* dated 16th February. It was bordered in black and had an illustration of the coffin lying in state at Windsor Castle. Marty scanned the article.

"We had better inform the squadron," Marty said.

"I will sail up the line and hail them," Richard said.

They went back on deck where Marty asked that the entire crew be assembled.

"I have grave news. His Majesty King George the third passed away on the 29th day of January. He was interred in St George's chapel in Windsor on the 16th of February. The prince regent has assumed the throne. God save The King!"

The men responded with a hearty 'God Save The King!'

"Set our colours to half-mast. Wolfgang make sail."

They sailed into Portsmouth and showed their number, a boat came out to meet them. A flag lieutenant resplendent in his gold braid came aboard.

"Compliments of the Port Admiral, Commodore. I have urgent messages for you."

He handed over a thick packet wrapped in waxed paper and sealed.

"They must be urgent if they have sent you out. Lieutenant Hardy, isn't it?" Marty said, recognising him. "Weren't you at the admiralty?"

"I was but have been the adjutant to Admiral Sheldon for the last six months or so."

"He's the port admiral now?"

"Yes, Sir."

"Do you need a reply?"

"I was told to have you sign for them and wait in case you needed to reply."

"Then allow me to read them and I will let you know." Marty turned to Wolfgang. "Captain Ackermann, will you accompany me?"

Marty and Wolfgang sat in Marty's cabin. Marty slit the seal and opened the packet. Inside were two sets of sealed orders and a letter.

Marty handed one set of orders to Wolfgang. He opened the other.

"Hmmm, this is very strange. I am to split the squadron in two. The Leonidas and Nymphe are to be refitted then join the Mediterranean fleet in Malta. Their excess marines to be retained aboard the other ships which are to be refitted and I am to source a troop carrier. I am to report to Admiral Turner at my earliest convenience. What do yours say?"

Wolfgang opened his and read them. "Basically that I am to take the Unicorn with the Endellion, and Eagle to Chatham and have them refitted. I am to take aboard the excess marines from the Leonidas and Nymphe. The crews can have shore leave. They are signed Secretary to the First Sea Lord."

Marty hmphed and opened the letter.

"Any more light on the situation?" Wolfgang asked.

"Not really. It's from Turner. It just says the situation has changed from our last communication and that they now need me and the SOF, strange that they have resurrected that title, to aid, covertly, an ally. For this all the ships will be refitted to look like civilian ships."

"I suppose that means the Unicorn will have to look like a frigate converted to a merchantman," Wolfgang said. "Anything else?"

"Not really, only that we can hire, or buy, a suitable troop ship."

"Angus and James to command?"

"Yes, get them onto the Unicorn. I am going to London once we get to Chatham."

Marty found Lieutenant Hardy.

"I hope you enjoyed looking around the Unicorn."

"I did thank you, Sir. She is impressive."

"I have an answer for my admiral. Please have this sent over the telegraph." He handed Hardy a sheet of paper. The lieutenant quickly read it to make sure he understood it. It simply said, "To Admiral James Turner. I will attend you in London. M."

"That is all?"

"That is all. We will set sail as soon as we have complied with the other orders."

Hardy looked a little miffed he wasn't being let in on the content, but he was too professional to ask.

Marty called an all-captains' meeting and when they were all assembled, he addressed them.

"Gentlemen, by now you have all received your individual orders. I wish I could shed more light on what we are going to be asked to do but I cannot because I do not know."

"Secret then," James Campbell, Captain of the Leonidas, said.

Marty smiled, "The fact that Admiral Turner has resurrected the Special Operations Flotilla tells us something. This is a job that no one else in the navy is either capable of, can or wants to do."

"Bugger, something fun comes up and we get sent to be messenger boys for the Mediterranean fleet," Andrew Stamp of the Nymphe said. The others laughed and James Campbell patted him on the back in consolation.

Marty had a sneaking suspicion that he would see more of those two in the future.

"Now to celebrate our comradeship, and the adventures we have had, Rolland has prepared a special dinner." Adam and the two youngest mids served glasses of semi-dry Madeira. The party had started. The mainbrace was spliced and the crews of all the ships were given a double ration of rum. Soon pipes and fiddles could be heard as the crew sang and danced.

Chatham on a cold March morning saw a coach and four, and several riding horses waiting on the dockside as Marty and the boys came ashore. The horses' breath steamed as they stood patiently waiting. Marty climbed the steps from his barge being careful not to slip on the green slim. The Shadows followed him. A hoar frost rimmed the windows of the coach and coated everything in ice. He was thankful that Adam had found his heavy winter coat, scarf, and gloves.

His coat of arms on the door told anyone that bothered to look that the coach was his. The door opened as he approached.

"Hello, husband," Lady Caroline said.

"Hello, wife." Marty climbed in and took her in his arms. Adam closed the door discretely after placing charcoal fired brass foot warmers inside.

Billy took the rumble seat at the back of the coach and Antton climbed up beside the driver. Adam climbed up next to Billy with a "budge up." Billy was armed with a vicious-looking short, barrelled blunderbuss, Adam and Antton sported rifles. They were all wrapped in heavy coats, scarves, gloves and woollen fisherman's hats.

"Can't you ride a horse?" Billy said.

"Not unless you can find another. They're all taken," Adam replied.

It was true. Matai, Garai, Rolland and Chin had mounted the horses. They rode with their rifles in hand, butts resting on their thighs. Without a command being given the coach set off.

"James Turner said you would arrive today," Caroline said.

"He probably received reports of our progress from every signal tower along the coast. Did you talk with him?" Marty said.

"Yes, he visited. Something is going on and he isn't saying anything."

"What he doesn't say is sometimes more important than what he does."

"Well, he did say that you would be home while all your ships were refitted." Caroline smiled at the thought of having her husband to herself for a while.

"Did he say how long that would take?"

"At least until the winter. He said the dockyards are busy, which means you will be here for Georgie's coronation."

Marty harrumphed, then said,

"I hear he isn't that popular, and he has gotten fat."

"He is almost as round as he is tall now. He eats prodigious amounts of food, and his health is poor. The people think he is a wastrel."

Marty didn't comment on that.

"When is the coronation?"

"The 1ˢᵗ of August at Westminster Abbey."

"Ugh, I will have to put on all the paraphernalia in the summer heat."

"You will survive. He has been a good friend to us."

"What else has he been up to?"

"He is trying to sue Caroline for divorce, she is refusing and is asserting her rights as Consort."

Marty winced at the thought of the tension that had to be causing.

"Ouch, that means he will have to go to parliament."

"Yes, but there is a fly in that ointment as well."

"Pray tell."

"The masses love her and despise him for his treatment of her," Caroline said sadly.

"Oh Christ, you mean she's become a folk hero?"

"Something like that."

"Then the politicians won't want to pass any bill he introduces to annul the marriage. Damn, this is going to be messy."

"James advises we stay at arm's length," Caroline said.

"That's easier said than done." Marty sighed.

"It certainly will be. Georgie has asked to see you."

Marty didn't say what he was thinking. Instead, he asked, "He knows I'm back then."

"Yes, he has had his agents keeping an eye on the telegraph as well."

They got to the London house and Marty changed out of uniform before sending a message to Turner that he would visit his house at nine o'clock the next morning. He then settled down to his mail. There were letters from Ryan Thompson concerning his holdings. From his brother about the Dorset estate. His sisters about their children and his regular letter from Katy Turner.

Then he turned one up with a royal seal on. It was from Prince George and written in his own scrawly hand.

My dear and loyal friend, Martin,

By now you should have heard of the death of my dear papa which has made me King. I never thought this day would come, but I suppose it was inevitable with his ill health and all. I actually never wanted it but as first born I have my duty. I am trying to sue Caroline for divorce. I never wanted to marry her in the first place but Papa insisted.

I am surrounded by idiots who would have me believe they are loyal. Please attend to me as I value your advice. Just come as soon as you can, I have left instructions for you to be admitted whatever I am doing.

It was signed, simply, *George.*

Caroline came into his study and saw the look of concern on his face. He handed her the letter.

"Oh Lord, you can't refuse this."

"I know, I had better get it over and done with."

Marty changed clothes to something more suitable for a palace visit and had his coach collect him. He wore a tricorn hat adorned with a feather and a coat with his honours emblazoned upon it.

His driver was stopped at the gates to St James's Palace.

"I've Viscount Stockley inside for an audience with the king," he heard his coachman say.

The guard stomped up to the coach door and opened it. Marty gave him his best officer's look. The man must have recognised him as he saluted and bowed as he closed the door before waving them through. A parade ground shout announced his arrival. They entered into the Colour Court and were met by footmen and a member of the royal household.

"My Lord Stockley, you are expected. Please come with me."

Marty wore no sword but that didn't mean he was unarmed. Far from it, his cane contained a blade, he wore his fighting knife behind his back and his navy-style queue contained several implements to be used in an emergency.

He followed the courtier who introduced himself as Sir John Dyer, Baronet, Equerry to the king. *In other words,* Marty thought, *the king's go-for.*

"The king is breaking his fast," Sir John said.

They entered the royal chambers and Marty had to control a gasp as he saw the spread laid out in front of George. There were two pigeons, three, inch-thick beefsteaks, a bottle of white wine, and glasses of champagne, port, and Brandy

"Martin! Good to see you. Sit, sit, have a glass."

"Thank you, your Majesty, but I would prefer a cup of coffee."

"Get Lord Martin a cuppa coffee!" George bellowed.

Sir John bowed and left.

"Good that's got rid of him for a bit," George said.

"You wanted to see me, Georgie." Marty relaxed into his chair.

"Yes, I miss your good advice when you are off having adventures. How was India, by the way?"

"India is in safe, if rather avaricious hands. It was as usual interesting, and Raffles has got Singapore established under the noses of the Dutch."

"Excellent, excellent." Georgie was working around to what he really wanted to talk about. "You know about the situation between me and Caroline. What do you think I should do?"

Marty steepled his fingers under his chin. He chose his words carefully.

"I believe that as she refuses to agree to a divorce that your only recourse is to try and get a bill through parliament."

Georgie nodded furiously around a mouthful of steak.

"However, it is my honest assessment that, due to her apparent popularity with the masses," this was an understatement of gigantic proportions as the general public adored her, "the politicians are unlikely to risk going against them and grant a divorce. My advice would be to keep her at arm's length as much as possible and keep her from appearing in public to prevent her stirring up further resentment. Remember as long as she is 'Queen' she is, to a large extent, beholden to do what you say."

"That's your honest assessment?"

"It is and I vow that I have your best interests at heart."

"I have no doubt of that, but damn, my father should never have made us marry."

"That is undoubtedly true, but it is what it is, and you have to work around it. It's a bit like escorting a convoy. The independent skippers want you to protect them but will be damned if they do what you say. So, you have to work around them."

"I hear what you say." Georgie looked at the door as if expecting Sir John to appear. "There is one more thing, I mean the coronation is costing more than parliament is willing to pay and my coffers are falling a bit short."

"You want a loan?"

"If you could."

The door opened and Sir John returned with a footman who carried a pot of coffee, cup and saucer, cream, and sugar.

"Just black please," Marty said, before the man asked.

"Will you be here for my coronation?" Georgie said, changing the subject.

"I will, the flotilla is being refitted for its next mission and I will be onshore until the autumn."

"Where will you go?"

Marty made a point of glancing at Sir John and replied, "I don't know yet. I must visit Admiral Turner for my orders."

"Will you be in London till then?" Georgie asked.

"We will spend the rest of this month (March) in London then Caroline wants to visit Cheshire. I will see my family in June then we will return to London in early July."

"We are having an Easter ball on April 1st. You, Caroline, and your children must attend."

Marty took that as a royal command and nodded his agreement.

Chapter 2: London

Marty sent a message to Beth to be in London for the ball. She was at the Secret Service Academy in Bedfordshire learning her chosen trade. Marty doubted they could teach her much, but the formalisation of what he taught her was probably not a bad thing. She would graduate next year and go into active service.

James was on shore leave and courting Melissa. She would, of course, accompany him to the ball. The twins, now fourteen, were old enough to go as well.

Constance, like Beth, was tall like her mother and growing into a beauty. She had no desire to emulate Beth, being more into animals. Marty suspected she would become an animal doctor.

Edwin was tall and a natural horseman. His ambition was to go into the cavalry. He was a good swordsman and rode with the hunt whenever he could. In India that meant hunting wild boar, but in England it would be deer or fox hunting. Marty didn't see the point in fox hunting. You couldn't eat it so why chase it for sport? Oh yes, he understood the argument concerning controlling them, as a fox in a henhouse would cause catastrophic damage. But wouldn't shooting them be easier and more humane? That is what they did on his land.

The prospect of a ball sent Caroline into a frenzy of shopping and dressmaking. Apparently, her entire wardrobe was out of date and had to be replaced. Marty braced his shoulders and went shopping for new suits before Caroline could intervene.

Martin's tailor was in Saville Row, and he walked into the shop with James and Edwin in tow. The proprietor, a busy, chalk-stained man wearing a Kippah, presented himself to him.

"My Lord, welcome to my humble shop. How can we help you."

Marty looked around. The shop was far from humble with oak panelling and bolts of cloth from all over the world neatly stacked on shelves.

"Mr Goldsmith, we are in need of new suits including ones suitable for attending a royal ball," Marty said.

"My Lord has been in the east?" Goldsmith said looking at their tans.

"India."

"For the ball, can I suggest that you have swallow-tailed jackets of black or dark blue, with pale yellow, rather than white, waistcoats that will show off your complexions, white silk shirts of the latest style, and cravats. The trousers should be white cashmere. I can also supply the latest in overcoats and gloves."

"That seems to be adequate," Marty said.

"Does my Lord want silver or gold buttons? May I say that gold would be more appropriate to his rank."

"Gold then."

"For day suits this is the latest fashion." He showed Marty a dummy fitted out with a colourful waistcoat, tailcoat and pantaloon trousers."

Marty ordered four suits in muted colours with silver buttons for daily use and dark blue suits for the ball. He allowed the boys to choose their own everyday suits. Then they had to be measured. Edwin was growing at a phenomenal rate, so the tailor made an allowance for that. James, like Marty, waited until his younger brother was done.

"I wish to be able to carry certain weapons without them causing unseemly bulges in our suits. Can they be accommodated?"

"What did Milord have in mind?" the tailor said, intrigued.

James held his coat open to show a pair of pistols holstered on his belt. "These and this." He turned to show the knife he carried on the back of his belt.

The tailor looked at Marty in shock and opened his mouth to say something when Marty opened his coat to show his pistols under his arms. Then turned around to reveal his fighting knife. Goldsmith's mouth snapped shut.

"It would be useful to have sleeves slightly looser than normal as well," Marty said.

"Who made those suits?" Goldsmith looked carefully at the cut and how it served to conceal the weapons.

"A chap in Calcutta," James said.

"A talented man, I would have him work for me."

He examined the cut of their jackets, noting the adjustment that had been made for Marty's Mantons and James' single-shot pistols.

"Do you normally go so heavily armed?" he said.

"Always unless we are going to a royal ball. Then we just carry the knives at the back," Marty said.

"If we are going to a normal ball, we might take a couple of stilettos in arm sheaths." James grinned.

"That would account for the loose sleeves?" Goldsmith said.

James nodded. Goldsmith stopped asking questions, he wasn't sure he wanted to know the answers to the ones in his head.

Measurements taken, they were told the suits would be ready for fitting in a week. Their next stop was to Lock and Co. Hatters in St. James's Street where Marty ordered beaver top hats for the three of them. Likewise, the hats would be ready for collection in a week's time.

The final stop was Wilkinson's Swordsmiths. Prince George had sent a message instructing Marty to go there but failed to say why or what for. He entered the shop with the boys on his heels and was recognised immediately. It was like they hadn't been away.

"Milord Stockley, we have been expecting you," the manager said with a bow. Marty raised an eyebrow.

"You have me at a disadvantage, as all I know is that I was instructed by His Majesty to visit."

The manager smiled gently and beckoned to a clerk who came forward carrying three long boxes and three shorter ones. He took a long box and checked the label before handing it to Marty. Marty opened it and inside was a beautiful small sword with a jewelled guard. The pommel was a ruby engraved with his coat of arms. On the ricasso had intertwined GR under a crown and the inscription *'Amicus Muse Fidelus'*.

"My faithful friend," Marty murmured.

James and Edwin opened theirs and they were similar to Marty's except their inscriptions said *'Pium Dison'*.

"My loyal godson," James translated.

The smaller boxes were addressed to Caroline, Beth and Constance and contained silver daggers each with similar inscriptions to the men's.

James had an inspiration and talked to the manager. He nodded as James told him what he wanted.

"How long?"

"A week, we have a spare blade that was made for your sister's dagger, the hilt and guard need to be made and the blade engraved."

James shook his hand sealing the order after writing a note.

"What was that?" Marty asked after they left the shop.

"A little something for Melissa," James replied.

Marty walked to Admiral James Turner's house which was a brisk fifteen minutes away. He knocked on the door and was admitted by his butler. Perseverance Hope, Percy, had been the admiral's steward when at sea, but had settled into the role of butler now James sailed a desk.

"Good morning, Lord Martin, the admiral is expecting you."

"Morning, Percy, lovely morning."

"It is, indeed, Sir."

Percy took Marty's hat and coat then led him into the admirals study which was a large comfortable room with club chairs as well as a desk. James was drinking coffee in one of the chairs. There was a pot and a second cup waiting for Marty.

"Good morning, Martin, welcome home," James said and stood to shake hands.

"Good morning to you too, James," Marty said, using his first name as they were both out of uniform. "I am very pleased to be back."

They sat and James poured Marty a coffee. Marty sipped it and said, "Blue mountain, from our estate?"

"Caroline gifted us with a regular supply."

"Aah, I remember: Christmas two years ago."

They sat in silence for a moment savouring the coffee and remembering Christmases past.

"I ought to bring you up to date," James said, breaking their revery. You know about the king?"

"Yes, visited him yesterday. He is fat and wants a divorce."

"He'll not get it."

"That's what I told him."

"Aside that, the politicians want a peace premium. They have reduced the navy to the point we can barely cover the trade routes, and the army has been decimated."

"Fools, don't they realise it's only the navy that keeps the empire together?" Marty scoffed.

"Not when there is money to be saved."

"Then that is what was going to happen to the squadron?"

"Yes, until George Canning intervened. He suddenly remembered our commitment to support the Greeks in their bid for independence."

"So, you resurrected the SOF to cover it."

"Yes, a flotilla sounds so much smaller than a squadron and those idiots don't know the difference."

"And I am to be the head of the flotilla?"

"Exactly, you became available after doing a splendid job in India and were the natural choice."

"But you still had to reduce the squadron."

"Only in appearance. The two ships that are on their way to the Mediterranean fleet will be at your disposal as they will be tasked with patrolling the Aegean out of Corfu. You and the SOF will be running around the islands and mainland training the Greek fighters."

"A marine captain could run that, why do you really need me?"

James smiled, "Counterespionage, there are factions in Greece that don't want independence from the Ottomans. They are the reason that the attempted rebellion in the north failed. They were feeding the Ottomans all the information they needed to squash it."

"That's the mission there. What is going on here?"

"There is a faction that is actively opposing our interference in any foreign affairs. Why? We aren't sure. They are members of the Whigs." James passed Marty a sheet of paper that was in code.

Marty scanned it, decoding on the fly.

"There are some interesting names on here, influencers."

"Yes. We would like to find out who they are talking to, but it would have to be handled very delicately."

"Can I make a suggestion?" Marty said.

"Suggest away!"

"Beth is not a known member of the service. She isn't on the payroll yet and we don't publicise who attends the academy as it officially doesn't exist. Under my guidance she could be an effective agent for this."

"Actually, that was what we had in mind. We need to make them think they are getting access to you through her."

That wasn't what Marty had had in mind, but it was a workable plan. James passed him an envelope.

"In here is an invitation to a party. There will be at least four of the suspects attending including Mr Gabriel Gershman, the youngest of the group."

Marty bristled, "She is to seduce him?"

James held his hand up. "She is to do whatever she deems necessary to gain his confidence."

Marty was mollified, a little. Beth wasn't twenty-one yet, in fact nineteen in October, and was still his little girl.

"Alright we can do it. She can stay in London when the rest of us go to Cheshire and Dorset. I will talk to her this evening."

Marty stood; it was time to leave.

"Will you be at the ball?"

"Yes, Juliette and I will be there."

A week later, Marty and the boys were back in Saville Row having their suits fitted. For speed all three were stood on low stools, dressed in their suits while tailors fussed around them making sure they fit in all the right places. That done, they picked up their hats and James picked up his parcel from Wilkinson's. The suits would be delivered to the house once they were ready.

It was the day before the ball. The suits arrived and triggered a dress rehearsal. Caroline had them all suited and booted. Beth arrived in time to have a dress made for her. Caroline and her daughters wore the daggers that Georgie had given them on garters around the thigh.

Melissa joined them, splendid in a lavender dress she had made for the occasion.

"Melissa, your outfit is incomplete," announced James when she lined up with the other ladies. Melissa looked confused until James presented her with a box tied with a ribbon.

"What?" she said. James gestured for her to open it. Beth and Constance crowded around to see what was in it.

"Oh! My!" she exclaimed as the silver-bladed dagger and kid skin sheath were revealed. She saw that it had been engraved in Latin, '*Il mio amore più caro*'.

"Now you are all suitably armed," James grinned.

Melissa knew exactly what he was talking about as she had seen the others fitting their daggers to their thighs with garters.

"I will have to find a garter then," she said. Edwin sniggered, earning him a casual clip around the ear from Marty.

Caroline intervened. "I can supply an appropriate method for carrying it and my dressmaker can make the hidden pocket for access. Now let me see how you all look."

She had the twins pair up for inspection, then James and Melissa. Finally, she had her and Marty stand in front of a huge mirror.

"Excellent, we all look positively splendid."

The next afternoon they prepared in earnest. Marty bathed and was shaved by Adam. His hair in a traditional sailor's queue. He wore his honours on a sash along with a gold broach in the shape of an epaulette with a star to signify his rank in the navy. His cravat was held by a diamond-headed pin of at least two and a half carats, and he had a gold full hunter watch and chain on his waistcoat.

He had his knife on the back of his belt and wore the short sword from Georgie. Apart from that he was unarmed and felt almost naked. James joined him similarly attired except he wore a gold pin that Melissa had given him.

"Where's Edwin?" Marty asked.

"Here, Papa." Edwin strode into Marty's rooms. His voice was breaking and he warbled between alto and tenor.

Marty inspected him.

"I bet you didn't inspect James," Edwin complained.

"James is Navy and knows how to dress."

Edwin harrumphed but submitted.

"Good, you both pass muster. Let's go down to the drawing room to wait for the women."

"Why are they always late?" Edwin said. He was having trouble with his sword which seemed to have a mind of its own and conspired to trip him up.

"Hold it by the pommel like this and stand upright. Then it will not tangle in your legs," Marty said. "Your mother is never late. She arrives precisely when she wants to."

"Why?"

"Because she wants to show us all off."

"Why?"

Marty sighed. "That is something you will discover for yourself as you get older."

They waited in the drawing room. Marty could see their coach waiting outside, the coachman patiently sitting on the driver's seat with Antton beside him. They were chatting about something. The coach rocked as Billy took the postern seat and placed a blunderbuss down by his feet.

He turned as the door opened and Caroline made her entrance followed by the girls. The array of jewels on show was breathtaking. Caroline and Beth being the most resplendent with Constance a more maidenly third. Melissa wore the jewels James had bought her and a circlet of silver with a central flower in sapphires that Caroline had lent her.

"Shall we go?" Caroline said.

Chapter 3: The Easter Ball

The ball was at St James's Palace of course. Their entrance, timed by Caroline to perfection. Beth, being single and unescorted, was immediately the centre of attention for all the young beaus and dandies. She had decided to be judicious in her choice of dance partners and proved to be, outwardly at least, immune to flattery. Caroline had to send for her to be presented to the king as their turn arrived.

The king, who looked slightly bored, looked up and saw them.

"Martin, Caroline, you light up the room with your presence!" he crowed as Marty bowed and Caroline elegantly curtsied. He clapped Marty on the shoulders, kissed Caroline on both cheeks, then turned his attention to the children, "And, my god! Bethany, you have grown into a beautiful woman!" Beth smiled winsomely at the compliment as she curtsied.

"Why thank you, Uncle Georgie," she said, causing the king to giggle.

He blew her a kiss then bent to look at the twins. "Constance, you are the prettiest young lady in the room. Edwin, as handsome as your father." He caught sight of James and Melissa who were next in line.

"And here we have James. Welcome, young man. Who is this beauty you have on your arm?"

"May I present Miss Melissa Crownbridge, your Majesty." James bowed.

Georgie tried to bow over her hand as she curtsied which made her blush.

"You have as good taste as your father. Another beauty." He all but leered.

Marty stepped in. "We thank you for your generous gifts, Your Majesty."

Georgie lent forward and horse whispered, "I bet those vixens are all carrying them right now, eh?"

"Indeed, they are, but I wouldn't try and find them if you value your fingers," Marty whispered back conspiratorially.

Georgie guffawed, sending ripples up and down his fat belly.

Marty bowed and moved on to allow the next in line to be presented.

Beth was glowing at the king's compliment. *Such a shame he is so fat!* she thought.

"Daddy, I will get something from the buffet then dance."

"Don't drink too much."

She gave him a look that made her the twin of her mother.

"As if I would."

In that he could trust her. She didn't like the effect wine had on her and limited herself to two or three glasses over an evening, preferring fruit juice. He watched her walk away. He had briefed her on her mission, and she had asked professional questions. She would receive a further briefing from a senior member of the Intelligence Service. But for now, she could be just Beth.

Beth had her evening planned out. She would eat a light meal from the buffet then dance the night away. As she approached the buffet, she was aware of a number of young men homing in on her. She ignored them and browsed the laden table for items for her plate. A terrine caught her eye and some slices of ham. A basket of bread, French baguettes, she broke off a chunk and spread it with butter. Spooned chutney and Indian style piccalilli on her plate then spotted a samosa.

Her plate full, she moved to take a seat at one of the many tables. She was joined by another two young women of around her age.

"Hello, what's your name? We haven't seen you at a ball before," one asked. She had brunette hair and wore a bonnet."

"Bethany Stockley. What's yours?"

"Abigail Southwell, Daddy is the member for Hampshire. What does yours do?"

"He is a commodore in the Royal Navy."

The other girl perked up, "Oh, Commodore Stockley! He's a viscount and a friend of the king."

"And who are you?" Beth said kindly.

"Clarissa Thompson-Holmes. My daddy is a member too."

"Does that make you a Lady?" Abigail asked.

"I am a 'Right Honourable', but I never use my title unless someone annoys me."

The girls giggled. Beth realised they were both less experienced in life than she was. She ate her meal and listened to their chatter about the other girls in the room and about the boys.

Good Lord! They are here looking for husbands, she realised. She had no such ambitions. She wanted to have her adventures first.

She finished her meal and looked up to see a number of young men waiting patiently for her to stand so they could approach and ask for dances.

"We had better let these boys dance with us before they burst," Beth said.

She stood. She was inches taller than Clarissa and a head taller than Abigail, and her tiara made her look even taller. She felt a touch on her shoulder and spun around ready to break the arm of whoever it was. She froze.

"Hello, Beth," a familiar voice said. *It can't be!*

She looked into his eyes.

"Sebastian?"

"The one and only. May I have this dance?"

She collected herself.

"Of course."

Behind her Clarissa and Abigail sighed as Beth stepped away on the arm of the handsome 'Major of Rifles'.

They danced a waltz. Her eyes never left his.

"I lost touch with you after Waterloo," she said.

"I went to South America to help with the revolution. When I came back, I was asked to join the Rifles by Wellington himself. He gave me the rank of Major. Now I am part of the king's bodyguard for the coronation."

"Have you married?"

"Me? No. What woman would have me."

"Oh, I don't know, you are reasonable to look at and have rank. Did I forget to mention you are the son of Lord Shaftesbury?" Beth teased.

"Ah, but I was spoiled as a husband at an early age by a siren."

"Were you?" she said her heart in her eyes.

"Martin, is that Sebastian Beth is dancing with?" Caroline said.

"Well, I'm damned, I believe it is."

He led them closer to the young couple, then felt Caroline resist.

"What is it?"

"Look at their faces."

"Oh, I see what you mean. I don't believe there is another person in the world as far as they are concerned."

He steered them away, *young people needed space,* he told himself.

Caroline giggled.

"What is it?" he asked.

"Don't you hear it? Hearts are breaking all around the room."

Beth forgot all about her dance card. A grenadier lieutenant, who she had promised a dance to, approached but when he saw who she was with did a smart about face and walked away.

Sebastian told her of his adventures in South America.

"How exciting! I was worried you had forgotten me."

"I never forgot you."

She giggled.

"But you did run away."

"I was afraid."

"Afraid? You? You aren't afraid of anything."

"You were fifteen and I was falling in love with you."

"Daddy would only have shot you a little bit. Anyway, I'm not fifteen anymore."

"No, you are not."

"I will be nineteen in October."

"I know and I will be here to celebrate your birthday."

"Aah," she said.

"You might not be here?"

"Well, you see, I've—"

"Followed your father's footsteps? I know."

"How?"

"His exposure to your father gave Wellington an idea."

"Oh no, you're not a—"

Sebastian raised one eyebrow in imitation of Marty,

"Special force. A rifle brigade that is specially selected and trained for fighting behind enemy lines. We work with the Intelligence Service much like Martin's Marines. One of my men visited the academy that doesn't exist and saw you there."

"I will have to shoot him," she giggled.

"No need. He was sworn to secrecy. We all had to sign a pledge before joining the brigade."

Beth spotted her parents standing at the buffet.

"Let's get something to eat."

"Prospective son-in-law at four o'clock," Marty grinned.

"Behave yourself, they just got reacquainted," Caroline scolded.

Marty schooled his features.

"Mummy, Daddy, look who I found."

Marty was about to say he thought it was the other way around when Caroline stood firmly on his foot.

"Hello, Lord Martin. A pleasure, Lady Caroline." Sebastian smiled as he saw Marty wince. He bowed over Caroline's hand.

"Hello, Sebastian," Marty managed through gritted teeth.

"Is something wrong, Sir?"

Caroline released the pressure.

"Just a pinching shoe," Marty said, firing Caroline a look. "You made Major."

"Of a special brigade," Beth said.

Marty raised an eyebrow. Beth giggled.

"Modelled after your marines, Sir. Wellington's idea. It seems enough of the Rifles were exposed to your way of working that he had no trouble at all in forming it."

"Where are you based?" Caroline asked.

"At St James's Palace at the moment, my unit is providing personal protection for the king until after the coronation. Then we will be based in Horse Guards."

"Are you on duty now?" Marty asked.

"No, but my men are."

"I spotted several who seemed to be particularly attentive."

"No doubt."

James Turner and his wife Juliette wandered over to join them. There were many bejewelled and titled ladies, and the place was chock full of aristocrats. But this little group shone. The king had retired leaving his guests to dance the night away, and that is just what they did.

Beth was floating on a cloud when they finally got home humming a tune and dancing up the stairs to her bedroom. Marty and Caroline exchanged a look that said it all. The twins just yawned and went to bed.

"Seems like love is in the air," Marty grinned.

"Well at least it's someone you approve of," Caroline said and kissed him on the cheek.

Marty frowned suddenly. "I hope this doesn't get in the way of her mission."

Marty needn't have worried. Come the morning Beth was all business at breakfast.

"I will get my briefing tomorrow. Gabriel Gershman is my subject."

"When is the party?" Caroline asked.

"Thursday."

"We will be in Cheshire then," Caroline sighed. In fact, the household was packing to decamp to the house in Cheshire with a view to leaving on Tuesday.

"That's as maybe, but right now it's time to go to church," Marty said after checking his watch. It was Easter Sunday, and the entire family would attend the service at Grosvenor Chapel. Marty made sure he had plenty of crowns and half crowns in his pocket for the collection and a couple of guineas for the donations box.

They dressed warmly and plainly. The girls wore bonnets, smaller than were fashionable and far more practical, hand muffs, and cover-ups (a fashionable coat of the time) to fend off the chill. The boys wore wool overcoats and top hats. The chapel was unheated, and the congregation kept their coats and hats on during the service.

The afternoon was spent at home. A simple lunch, they felt no need to follow the Georgian tradition of indulgence, and dinner with the Shadows and their wives. Rolland and the cook worked together to provide a delicious three-course meal.

Fish Soup with saffron and anis

Roast rib of beef on the bone cooked rare in the middle
Roast potatoes and honey roasted parsnips, carrots, and braised
kale

Lemon posset or crème catalana

A delicate dry rose wine from Provence accompanied the soup, a
robust Côtes de Bourg Bordeaux with the beef, and an orange
muscat sweet wine from Italy with the desert.

Chapter 4: Cheshire

The household arrived in Cheshire. The convoy of two carriages and three wagons escorted by the Shadows on horseback rolled in late on Thursday. The resident staff were assembled to greet the family. Marty and Caroline greeted each in person. Before that though a brindled tornado hit Marty as Troy, still nimble despite his years, greeted him. From then on, he never left his side.

Unpacking took no time at all; the staff efficiently unloaded the wagons, and their personal luggage was whisked up to their rooms and unpacked before dinner. Ryan and Louise met them inside and the twins immediately asked about their cats.

"They are in their enclosure. You can visit them in the morning." The cats in question were a pair of Leopards, Rhaja and Princess, that Marty had taken in as cubs when he was forced to shoot their mother in Ceylon. The twins had adopted them, and they had grown up together. The twins were impatient but their parents were adamant. They would have to wait until morning.

Marty was woken at dawn when the twins appearing in their bedroom, fully dressed.

"I suppose you two want to go and meet your cats?" he whispered so as not to wake Caroline. The twins nodded vigorously.

"Meet me downstairs." He rose and quietly dressed. After he left, Caroline smiled as she snuggled his pillow.

Matai had miraculously appeared along with Chin and were waiting with the twins in the hall. Ryan came out from his study pulling on a coat. A footman stood waiting with Marty's coat, scarf and gloves. Marty didn't say a word. He was used to the shenanigans of his household.

The cat's enclosure was at the side of the house and was almost an acre in size. It was surrounded by a stout wire fence and had a gate where their keeper (one of the grooms) could feed them.

As they approached Edwin and Constance started to call in Hindi using a strange musical cadence. There were answering roars from deep in the enclosure. The twins continued to call and suddenly the cats appeared running flat out towards the gate.

Before Marty or anyone could stop them, the twins opened the gate and rushed in towards their pets.

Marty reached for his gun and clicks told him that Chin and Matai were ahead of him. He need not have worried, the cats greeted the children by brushing up against them and when Edwin said something, Rhaja put his front paws on his shoulders and rubbed faces with him.

Marty and the boys relaxed. Ryan who hadn't moved said, "Those cats came and looked for the twins every day."

Collars and leads appeared, and the twins walked out of the enclosure, their cats beside them.

"Where are you going?" Marty asked.

"Just for a short walk," Constance said.

"Not too far, Chin and Matai will go with you." He said more for the comfort of anybody that happened across than for the twins protection.

It was as if they had not been away. Breakfast included his beloved black pudding, fried crisp on the outside in lard, bacon made from pork belly, eggs fresh from the hens, kidneys, and toast. Everything was sourced from the estate. Ryan and Louise joined them.

Louise only had a croissant and some jam on her plate, and she waited until Marty and Caroline had filled plates on front of them before saying, "I have some news."

Caroline immediately looked at her closely. Marty just said around a mouthful of black pudding, "What's that?"

"I am expecting a baby."

Caroline crowed joyfully and went around the table to hug her. Marty went to Ryan and shook his hand. "Well done!"

"How long?" Carline asked.

"Three months and a week."

Marty realised then what he had noticed when they first saw them. She was glowing. The women were deep into a discussion on pregnancy, so Marty and Ryan moved to sit opposite each other.

"We have been trying since you left for India, and she lost a couple before this one stayed put," Ryan said. "The doctor said it was because of the wounds she had sustained in the past."

Marty felt a pang of guilt as he felt responsible for them.

"Anyway, it is all good now. Everything has progressed as normal."

Ryan ate some of his breakfast which pointedly did not include black pudding.

"The estate and associated businesses are in good shape. We reduced the sheep flocks when the war ended as we anticipated a drop in the wool price. We have increased the production and processing of pork and our charcuterie is in high demand since we employed a former French soldier and his wife who had been charcutier in Lyon before the war. It would be even better if we could get the products to London faster. The cattle herd has been improved with the introduction of Guernsey bulls. Milk production is up, and the dairy is producing cheese which sells for a good price.

"Do you supply the royal household?" Marty asked.

"Why, yes we do."

"Then I probably sampled it at the king's Easter ball."

"Grain production was low last year, so we held back on selling until the price rose in the new year. We managed to make a small profit."

"It all sounds like the new practices are paying off."

"They certainly are. Do you want to do a tour of the estate?"

"Let's leave that to tomorrow. I would like to walk a few hedgerows this afternoon. I miss the countryside. Oh, and while I think of it, Edwin will want to join a local hunt."

"There is one at Chelford. I will write him a letter of introduction as I know the estate manager there."

After breakfast Marty, James and Edwin armed with shotguns and escorted by Troy and Bert Scriven, one of the estate's keepers, and his spaniels, left the house. They were looking for game for the pot. Marty had always instructed that the rabbits on the estate be left for the tenants and workers. Ryan also let them take pigeons. Game, however, was the preserve of the household. Woodcock, pheasant, hare, duck and deer were carefully managed by a team of keepers who kept the predators under control.

"Do we suffer much from poachers?" Marty asked Bert.

"Not since Mr Ryan did make an example of the last one we caught. Had him pressed into the marines he did. Silly bugger was shipped off on a ship to China."

The spaniels were ranging ahead, and a hare shot out of the undergrowth. James beat Marty to the shot and brought it down cleanly. A pheasant rose and Edwin took it with a single shot as well.

"Yer boys be fair shots, Milord," Bert said.

"They had plenty of practice in India."

The spaniels brought back the kills. Troy looked on as if it was below him.

"Your dog sired a litter on my bullmastiff bitch. They be seven weeks old now. Would you be wanting one?"

Marty had missed having a dog along on the last trip and Troy was frankly too old to come along on the next one. A cross between him and a bullmastiff should result in an awesomely powerful and intelligent dog.

"You have a male spare?"

"Two, you can see them this afternoon if yer wants."

They returned with four braces of pheasants and a pair of hares which were duly delivered to the kitchen. After they cleaned their guns, Marty went with Bert to his home. Troy of course followed on.

Bert had an estate house a half mile away and as they approached his bullmastiff greeted them at the gate. Troy looked interested in her, but she let him know in no uncertain terms that she wasn't interested in him or him getting close to her pups.

The pups were a variety of colours, some brindled others not. At that age all their ears were floppy. They were a noisy aggressive bunch.

"Six bitches and two dogs," Bert said.

Marty could see the boys as they were a bit bigger than the females, more muscled even at that age. He stepped into the pen. The female wandered off. She was fed up with the boisterous pups who were weaned off her milk now. One of the boys caught Marty's eye. He was standing his ground in front of him and growling.

"You're a feisty one." He took a knee in front of him.

The rest of the pups took the opportunity to tug at his coat and he felt a nip on his leg. He went to bat the offender away, but the boy stepped in and chased it off. He came back in front of Marty and sat his head to the side.

"Just like your father," Marty murmured and reached out so he could smell his hand. The pup smelt him then moved in closer. Marty rubbed his head.

"Your name is Hector, son of Troy," Marty said and picked him up.

"He be right for you," Bert said.

"He chose me," Marty laughed.

They returned home. Troy gaining new energy as he played with the pup in front of the fire. Caroline arrived and sat in a chair before saying anything.

"A new puppy." It was a statement not a question.

"Hector."

"A son of Troy, interesting. Who was the mother?"

"Bert Scriven's bullmastiff," Marty said almost too casually.

"Does James know?"

"Yes, he is looking at a bitch from the same litter."

"Oh. I thought you would go back to Holland for another shepherd."

"I was thinking about it, but this pup will suit just as well."

Caroline wasn't fooled.

"Softy, you just wanted one of Troy's sons."

James didn't take a pup from the same litter as he found out that Troy had been busy and there was another litter with an Irish setter mother. He fell in love with a boy with a long brindled coat, big brown eyes and very sharp puppy teeth.

The pups met and played ferociously under the fatherly gaze of Troy who decided they should get on with it. One thing he noticed was that Hector would chase anything. Shadows, motes of light, a leaf, a bit of paper. He had an incredibly strong hunting instinct. He also had a good nose like his father and could track down a treat wherever Marty hid it.

He trained the pup from day one and soon Hector would sit, stay and follow. He also trained him to bite using a rag. James' pup though smaller and more finely built, joined in the training keenly and could play tug with the best of them.

Caroline brought herself up to date with her businesses, spending long hours ensconced in her study with Louise. Together they plotted and schemed, identifying new business opportunities and ways to beat the opposition. Louise, like any ex-spy would, had created a network of informants and there wasn't much going on in the world of commerce that she didn't know about. Louise was also a part time instructor at the academy and had been involved in Beth's preparation for her mission.

As Caroline wouldn't be accompanying Marty on his next mission, she was looking forward to working with Louise and being able to support her during her pregnancy. One of their projected new markets was what Louise liked to call, "transportation for the masses." This was currently limited to horse-drawn trams and the use of rail wagons to move coal and ore from mines also powered by horses or static steam engines. A certain Mr Trevithick in Cornwall had changed all that with his self-propelled steam engine. Even though it blew up, the principle was world changing and they wanted in on the start of it. They were secretly funding several engineers around the country who were trying to solve the problem of steam-driven transport. Including a young Scott called George Stephenson.

Marty spent several days reading the latest farming periodicals and discussing with Ryan further improvements. Mechanisation was high on their list of things to consider. How to mechanise without driving people off the land was a major problem that would have to be solved.

"There are jobs that are really manpower intensive which we are already seeing changes," Marty said. Just the year before, the iron plough with interchangeable parts had been introduced making a big difference in the cost of ploughing. "If there was a horse-drawn scythe, it would save a huge amount of manpower that we have to dedicate to harvesting in the summer that could be used for other things."

"That's true. During harvest every man who can hold a scythe is drafted in. All the women are in the fields with sickles stacking the sheaves. Then they all take up flails and thresh the grain once it's dry enough. All the time they are doing that they could be out preparing the ground for the next crop. There just aren't enough ploughmen," Ryan said.

Chapter 5: Dorset

The months of April and May flew by and then they were off again heading to Church Knowle, a trip of a mere two hundred and fifty miles. At an average speed of eight miles an hour they could cover around eighty miles a day. It was backside numbing and uncomfortable even with the improved roads and a modern, sprung coach.

After overnight stops at two coaching inns and innumerable changes of horses, they arrived in Wareham for their final stop at the Red Lion. Marty felt drained and he knew that Caroline felt the same. The twins were still sulking from having to leave Rhaja and Princess behind. James was the only happy one as he and Melissa got to spend time together.

They received the usual effusive welcome from the innkeeper and his wife. They ordered hot baths, a meal and planned a quiet evening. It was not to be. Word of their arrival spread like wildfire and the local constable turned up.

"Is there something I can do for you?" Marty asked the man stood before him wringing his hat on his hands.

"Well, Sor, it be like this, the magistrate has fallen off his horse and there baint another within thirty odd mile. The nearest one being over yonder in Dorchester."

"Is he disabled?"

"Aye, Sor, broke his back he 'as."

"What do you want me to do?"

"Well, what with you being a Lord and an officer like, we was hoping you could hear a couple of cases and clear out the local jail as it's gettin' fearful crowded."

Marty sighed, he was quite entitled to act as a magistrate as he was a landowner in the area and a Lord to boot. Caroline smiled at him encouragingly. Then he had a thought.

"Why isn't Bankes doing this?"

The constable coughed and shuffled his feet.

"Come on, man, out with it!" Marty snapped, quite out of patience.

"Well, Sor, I don't like to speak bad of anybody but his Lordship doesn't have all his faculties and his son ain't the sharpest tool in the box."

Caroline hid a snigger behind a handkerchief and Marty had a coughing fit. Marty had several run-ins with the Bankes family over the years. Old man Bankes must be over seventy now and it was quite conceivable that he was senile.

"I will take the bench after we have settled in Church Knowle. Set the assises for Monday starting at ten."

"Thankee, Sor, I mean Milord."

Caroline burst into giggles after the poor man left.

"That was priceless," she spluttered.

Marty agreed, but the thought of standing judgement over his fellow man sobered him. Then he realised that he did it every day aboard ship, so this couldn't be much different.

The house at Church Knowle was just the same as the last time they were there. His brother Arthur and his wife met them at the door. Forewarned, their rooms were already prepared. The servants looked after the unpacking. Caroline told them what the sheriff said once they were inside.

"Old man Bankes has been going downhill for the last two years. They found him wandering around the village in his nightshirt last week and he didn't know where he was. The sheriff took him home," Arthur said.

"What about his son?" Marty said.

"Archibold? Thick as two short planks. Gordon says if brains were gunpowder, he couldn't blow his nose."

"That bad?"

"All he can do is ride that palfrey of his."

Marty took one of the saddle horses and rode into Corfe Castle. The ruin of the fortress looming above him on its hill. He looked up at the near vertical slope and could understand why it had been built there and how it had been once the strongest fortress in England. If you could get up the slope you would be faced with a sixty-foot-high wall.

He passed the stream down on his left that was called the valley. Smoke drifted up from the chimneys of the small terrace of houses where one of his uncles lived. He would be working at the mine in Norden at this time and his wife had passed a couple of years ago. The Bankes' house was further along on the far edge of the village. As he rode, he pondered on the legend of brave Dame Mary Bankes who had held the castle with thirty men against Cromwell's army only losing it when one of her own betrayed her. She was supposed to still haunt the ruins.

He tied his horse at the hitching post outside the house and knocked on the door. A man answered and Marty handed him a visiting card.

"My Lord, please, come in. His Lordship is in the drawing room." He looked embarrassed, "I'm afraid he is not having a good day today."

"Tell me," Marty said, "how bad is he?"

"That you can judge for yourself, Sir."

He let him into the room. Bankes was sitting in an armchair with a blanket over his lap. He was staring straight ahead and did not seem to be aware that Marty was there. Marty moved to stand in front of him and knelt on one knee to be at his eye height. The old man looked at him for a second then returned to staring into space.

Marty stood and walked to the door where the servant was waiting.

"I've seen enough. Where is his son?" Marty said as he left the house.

"Out riding, Sir."

Marty nodded and mounted. He kicked his horse to a trot and started for home. He had just reached the crossroads to turn to Church Knowle when a horse galloped past him. It was riderless and was heading towards Corfe. Fearing the rider had been thrown and was hurt he cantered in the direction it had come from, towards Studland.

In five minutes, he spotted a figure walking towards him dressed in a red coat. He slowed his horse to a walk.

"I say! You there! Have you seen a horse?" the man cried.

"One galloped past me heading towards Corfe."

"Oh. He's heading home then."

"Were you thrown?"

"Lord no. Stopped for a pee and a bird spooked him while I was at it." He smiled, "Always was skittish." He looked at Marty, "Don't think we've met, Archibald Bankes."

"Martin Stockley, can I offer you a ride home?"

"That would be capital, these boots ain't meant for walking."

Archibald climbed up behind Martin and they set off at a walk towards Corfe.

"Stockley Eh? You the chap that owns Church Knowle?"

"Yes, that's me."

"I knew your sister when I was younger, she was a maid at our house."

"She's come up in the world since then," Marty said dryly.

"I'd say!" There was silence for a bit then. "How did you go from clay miner's son to being a, what is it? Viscount?"

Marty decided not to react to the indelicate question and dump Archibald on his arse and said, "Good fortune, the navy and the love of a good woman."

Archibald prattled on. *He doesn't have an intelligent thought in his head!* And it was with some relief that they pulled up in front of his house. Archibald slid off the horse and held out his hand which Marty leaned over and shook.

"Can I offer you a glass?" Archibold offered, somewhat hopefully.

"No thank you, I need to get home."

Monday came and Marty arrived at the assises at nine in the morning and asked for the list of cases to be tried. He took over an office and examined the list. There were three men charged with drunkenness, two for fighting, a poacher, and a horse thief.

A horse thief? In Dorset?

Marty sat back. Dorset was made up of small villages and towns, apart from Dorchester and Bridport which were bigger. A horse thief would have to travel a significant distance to dispose of his ill-gotten steed or it or the brand would be recognised.

"Milord, the assises will open in ten minutes," a bailiff said from the door.

Marty rose and proceeded to the courtroom. Everybody stood when he entered and sat after he took his seat. A bailiff stood and called, "The court is in session. Milord Stockley presiding."

"Bring in the first defendant."

After he had dealt with the drunks, brawlers and poacher, the alleged horse thief was brought in. He was a young man and looked very frightened.

"What is your name?" Marty said.

"Arnold Cooper, Milord."

"Arnold, you are charged with horse theft. How do you plead?"

"I didn't do it, Milord."

"I will enter a plea of not guilty."

"Is there anybody representing you? A solicitor?"

"No, Sir."

"This is a very serious charge and the punishment, if you are proven guilty, will be an extended time in gaol or even death by hanging. Who is prosecuting this case?"

"I am, Milord," a cloaked gentleman said.

"And you are?"

"Eustus Filton."

Marty checked the notes he had been given.

"It was your horse he allegedly stole?"

"Yes, Milord."

"What evidence do you have?"

"The horse went missing and we found it in his barn."

"In his barn?"

"Aye."

"Don't you think it odd that he stole a horse and hid it in his own barn?"

"No, Milord, he always coveted her."

"Were there any other witnesses to the horse being found?"

"My two farm hands who was with me when we found it."

"I would like to hear what they have to say. Bailiff, please bring them to the court."

Marty turned back to Filton.

"Tell me. When did you notice the horse was missing?"

"When we went to feed her."

"We?"

"Me and my daughter."

"Your daughter, is she here?"

"That's her, over there in the gallery."

"Miss, please come down." Marty beckoned to her.

She was a pretty girl. Modestly dressed and it was obvious she had been weeping.

Marty looked at her kindly.

"Your name?"

"Lucy, Milord."

"You were with your father when he discovered the horse was stolen?"

"I was."

"Do you normally accompany him when he feeds the mare?"

"No, Sir."

"Why did he ask you to accompany you on this occasion?"

"Milord—" Filton tried to interject.

"Let her answer," Marty said sternly.

"I don't rightly know, he were angry that I had met Arnold while I were at the market."

Filton opened his mouth and Marty closed it with a look.

"Did you often meet Arnold at the market or other places?"

"We did and Arnold was going to ask my father if he could court me."

"You wanted that?"

"I did, Milord." She looked across at Arnold and the two exchanged a look that could only be seen as yearning.

"Tell me, when did you tell your father?"

"I didn't, Milord, I told me mum."

A commotion saw the bailiff return with the two farmhands.

"They were in the pub. Had florins to spend," he reported.

"Farmhands with florins to spend?"

"Aye, Sir. The landlord was complaining because he couldn't change them."

"You two step forward!" Marty barked in his quarterdeck voice.

The men looked terrified. Marty glared at them. One was visibly shaking.

"Bring me the bible," Marty said.

The book was provided.

"You, hold the bible and swear to tell the truth," Marty told the shaking man.

The man did as he was told. Marty glared at him bringing the full force of his authority down on him.

"Now, for the sake of your soul, you will answer my questions honestly. What is your name?"

"'arry, Milord."

"Tell me, Harry, where did you and that fellow there get those florins?"

"Mr Filton did give them to us, Milord."

"That is far more money than any farmhand has ever been paid. Why did he give it to you."

Harry's shaking increased and he looked stricken.

"I remind you that your soul is in peril if you perjure yourself."

"I'm sorry, Mr Filton!" Harry cried. "It were so we would say Arny stole his mare."

"Arny didn't steal it?"

"No, Milord, we did put it in his barn as Filton told us to."

"You can't believe them over me!" Filton shouted.

Marty sat back and gestured to the constable.

"Place Mr Filton under arrest for perjury and false witness."

"One last question, Harry. When did Filton order you to do that?"

"After his missus did tell him about Arny and Lucy. He were furious."

"Why?"

"He said he wouldn't have the son of Cliff Cooper marry his girl."

He turned to Arnold.

"Was there bad blood between your father and Mr Filton?"

"Aye, Milord, it went back to when they were lads. Something to do with a girl."

"Thank you, that provides the motive."

Marty made a note on the paper he had been recording the case on.

"Arnold Cooper, you are found not guilty of the charge. If I were you, I would marry Lucy as soon as her mother gives her permission. Her father is going to be indisposed for quite some time. You are free to go."

The trial of Filton was a formality as all the evidence had already been provided. Marty sentenced him to five years in Portland Prison.

On his way out of the court Arnold and Lucy approached him.

"Lord Stockley, can you spare a moment?" Lucy asked.

"Yes of course."

"We wants to thank you."

"No need, I'll not see a man punished for a crime he didn't commit."

"Lucy's dad were banking on Mr Hardwood being on the bench. He wouldn't have asked questions like you did," Arnold said.

"Wouldn't he?"

"No, he were often worse for wear as it were, Sir."

"Was he? Well, we will have to see about getting a new magistrate appointed. Now you two get along. You have a long life ahead of you."

Over dinner Martin was quizzed about his day. He told them and they were first shocked then amused by Filton's duplicity.

"Hardwood was not a good magistrate, but he was all we had," Arthur said.

"You know you qualify for being a magistrate," Marty said.

"Me?"

"Yes, you are a landowner with an independent income. That's all you need."

"I don't need to be a Sir or Lord?"

"Not under British law."

Alfred looked thoughtful and Marty let him think it through. He knew he would do the right thing.

Caroline smiled at the sight of Marty's older brother pondering following his youngest brother. The irony was not lost on her.

"Will Filton still have a farm when he gets out of gaol?" James said.

"That's another thing we need to consider. His wife and daughter are living there and Lucy will be marrying Arnold who has the neighbouring farm."

"Wouldn't it be more efficient if it was all one farm?" James said.

Caroline's eyes lit up. "That would be so romantic," she looked at Marty, "we could give Arnold the money to buy the farm off his mother-in-law."

"Lend dear," Marty corrected her as he knew that giving money would be seen as charity and not acceptable.

"At no interest of course."

Marty and Caroline visited Lucy's mother May. At one time she had been as pretty as Lucy but time and, as they found out, an abusive husband had taken its toll. She was all for selling the farm to Arnold but was worried what her husband would say when he returned.

"Do you want him back?" Caroline asked.

"I can do without his rough handling," May said.

Marty noted the look on Caroline's face.

"Would you mind if I searched for papers? Deeds and the like?" he said to May.

There was a deed that Marty found in a pile of papers stuffed into a drawer. It was in her father's name. No will was found but as she was an only child, she would have inherited it.

"Did you get married in church?" Marty asked.

"Oh no, we just jumped a broom," May said.

Caroline turned to him, "Why? Is that important?"

"There won't be any record of the marriage so legally May is the owner as only by marriage does the husband take ownership of her goods. It's the difference between local custom and the law of the land."

"Are ye sayin' tha' the farm be mine?"

"Yes, to do with as you will."

"Then when the kids get hitched, I will give it to them. That'll show that oud bastard."

Chapter 6: Consolidation

They returned to London in early July. Marty had tasked Fletcher to find him a suitable troop ship. He had talked with Angus Fraser and between them they had come up with a specification. Fast enough to keep up with the other ships of the flotilla, strongly built with enough room for one hundred sailors and sixty marines and davits for six landing boats. They eventually found a newly-built three-masted barque.

Marty visited the dock where the ship was tied up. She had been built by Wells, Ingram and Green at Blackwall but the person who had commissioned her had gone broke, so she was up for sale.

"Good-looking ship, nice lines, plenty of breadth and lots of space," Marty concluded after walking her decks.

"She will take sixteen twelve-pound longs without cluttering the deck and still have room for six sets of davits."

"Her deck can be reinforced for the guns and the davits seated on the ribs which can be braced with iron stretchers from one side to the other," Angus said.

"I will ask the admiral to buy her. Any ideas for a name?" Marty said.

"Well," Fletcher said, "Artemis is the Greek goddess of the hunt and Amphitrite the goddess of the sea."

"They have been used already," Marty said.

"Then how about Neaera? She was a sea nymph," Fletcher said.

"I didn't know you were a Greek scholar."

"I've read the Iliad a half dozen times."

"The Neaera she is then," Marty said when Angus gave his approval. "I will leave you two to commission the modifications."

Turner was waiting for Marty to find a ship and was prepared with a budget from Canning. Marty met Turner at his house.

"I will buy her in immediately, but she will not appear on the navy list. As to that all the SOF ships have been sold off."

Marty looked surprised. Turner grinned.

"They were sold to a secret purchaser."

"A very secret purchaser?"

"Yes."

"The Intelligence Service has its own navy now?"

"We have a number of assets that are available for use by our agents."

"Spoken like a politician." Marty applauded. "Where does that leave us if we are captured?"

"You will be issued Letters of Marque which are only to be used when you are in dire need."

"That will have to do as I have no desire to be hung as a pirate."

Turner nodded and continued. "Canning is consolidating the different intelligence units into one, under his control."

"What does Wellington think of that?"

"He is all for it. Sees it as the way forward."

"And you?"

"It makes sense and I have always worked closely with George."

"And my position?"

"Don't worry about that, he holds you in the highest esteem."

Marty didn't say anything, politicians changed their minds as circumstances dictated. Canning was one of the more consistent ones for sure, but he was a politician all the same.

"The new department is organised into domestic and overseas intelligence branches. I am the head of the overseas branch. You are the head of my mobile unit," Turner said.

"The SOF."

"Exactly and other assets."

"But I will be tied up in Greece."

"To an extent. Once you have things up and running you can take on other tasks. We will talk again when you return for the coronation."

Marty pondered this and foresaw a busy future.

"Where does Beth sit in this?" he asked.

"At the moment she is destined for the domestic branch. But I foresee her moving over to us at some time. What with her mastery of languages and all that."

"I will see her this afternoon. Can she talk to me about her mission?"

"Naturally. That reminds me all operatives and members of the new organisation are required to sign one of these."

He handed over a sheet of velum.

"Velum?"

"Lasts forever."

"Very symbolic." Marty read it. It was a pledge to secrecy.

"Do I sign in blood?"

Turner chuckled. "Nothing so dramatic, ordinary ink will do." He passed over a pen already loaded with ink and Marty signed. Then looked thoughtful.

"What happens to all our ranks if the ships are no longer part of the navy?"

"Wondered when you would ask that. You are all entered onto the navy books as active on HMS Silent. It's a fictional ship that gives you sea time."

Marty went from Turner's to his bank in the city. He met with the manager and went over his accounts. He was getting a little over one thousand pounds a year from the navy as a commodore plus extras for 'special duty'. His estates netted him in excess of fifteen thousand pounds a year after taxes. Caroline's enterprises were making a cool twenty-five thousand a year. He was immensely rich by anybody's standards, but the money meant little. As far as he was concerned as long as he could look after his family and people, he had enough. The rest was just keeping score.

"I want a foundation set up with ten thousand pounds for the pensions of the workers on my estates. It is to be invested in the five percent bonds. The bank will manage it. Trustees are Ryan and Louise Thompson."

"Yes, Milord. Do you want to keep your charitable donations the same?"

"The same charities but increase them by ten percent."

"Your wealth has increased. We have invested in gold, the Lloyds register, increased your holdings in the East India Company, and in engineering companies. You now have interests in two hundred companies under the pseudonym of Bridport Investments. Some of which may make a profit. Then there is the loan to the crown, will that bear interest?"

Marty smiled. "No it won't. We invest in the future, those companies are all led by men of vision. Some will make a difference and others will fail. It is the way of the world."

He stood. "If there is nothing else, I will take my leave."

Marty got a hackney carriage home and saw a carriage he recognised parked outside. The door opened when he was halfway up the steps and Adam said, "The Contessa Evelyn and her husband are visiting."

Evelyn was his first love and he had known her for, *my god, is it twenty-five years already!* He went into the drawing room. There was Evelyn. Petite, beautiful and as bright as the sun as she laughed at something Caroline said. Her husband Arthur, a brigadier in the Lifeguards, stepped forward and shook his hand.

"Martin, how are you?"

"I'm very well, Arthur, how are you and the children?"

Evelyn and Arthur were married just after Marty and Carline and had three children, the oldest of which was in the navy as a newly-made lieutenant. Their two youngest were sat talking to the twins.

Evelyn turned when she saw Caroline look up and stood. Marty embraced her and kissed her on the cheeks French style. Caroline smiled indulgently. They sat and caught up. Marty was sad to hear that her father was not well and promised to visit him. The count had started his career when he sponsored him as a midshipman, and he loved him like his own father.

First though they had to be fitted with his ceremonial robes. That meant obeying the command from the earl marshal which had been delivered to their home. It read:

THESE are to give notice to all Peers at the proceedings to His Majesty's Coronation, that the Robe or Mantel of the Peers be of Crimson Velvet, edged with Miniver, the Cape furred with Miniver Pure, and powdered with Bars or Rows of Ermine, according to their Degree, viz.

> Barons, Two Rows.
> Viscounts, Two Rows and a Half.
> Earls, Three Rows.
> Marquesses, Three Rows and a Half.
> Dukes, Four Rows.

Their under-habits of very rich White Satin, laced with Gold.
White Silk Stockings and White Shoes.
The Swords in Scabbards of Crimson Velvet appendant to a Belt of the same.

Their Coronets to be of Silver Guilt; the caps of Crimson Velvet, turned up with Ermine, with a Gold Tassel on the Top, and no Jewels or precious stones are to be set or used in the Coronets, or Counterfeit Pearls instead of silver balls.

Marty and Caroline visited Ede and Ravenscroft where they acquired appropriate robes for their rank. The rules were strictly enforced, and no deviation was allowed. Caroline was told that she wasn't allowed to embellish the Coronets with real jewels so she would have to settle for earrings and a necklace of diamonds.

The next day they got a letter telling them that the coronation had been postponed to August 1821. Marty knew that this was because of the divorce proceedings going through parliament.

They also received their tickets to the coronation which were individually numbered, named, and signed.

"I'm number 2032 and you are 2033," Caroline said.

"Probably in order of precedence," Marty replied from behind his newspaper which was full of the coronation and the cost of it. "It says here that it's going to cost more than two hundred and thirty thousand pounds."

"That's an awful lot. How much came from parliament?"

"One hundred thousand."

"Where on earth did Georgie find the rest?" Caroline said then gave Marty a sharp look as his tone was too bland. "Did you lend him money?"

Marty looked bashful and said, "He asked me outright, how could I refuse?"

"How much?"

"Only fifty."

"Fifty thousand?"

"Against his personal note."

Caroline left the room, shaking her head and muttering something about a fool and his money.

Marty visited the de Marchet's house to see how the count was doing. He was admitted and greeted by the countess.

"He is in his bed," she said.

"What is wrong with him?" Marty said.

"I don't think the doctors really know. They bleed him and he gets no better."

Marty frowned; he didn't like the sound of that at all.

"Can I have the use of one of your servants?"

"Mai oui. But why?"

"I want Shelby to look at him and he is at his house in Harley Street."

A servant was dispatched by hackney and returned within the hour with Shelby and his wife Anabelle.

Marty and the countess took them up to the count.

"Martin! I thought I heard you downstairs," he said then arched in pain.

"This is my physician Shelby and his wife Annabelle who is also a doctor. I want them to take a look at you."

"Where is the pain?" Shelby said, moving in confidently and professionally.

"Here, and right through to the back and down into my groin," the count said and pointed to the offending area.

Annabelle and Shelby exchanged a look and she nodded.

Damn they don't even need to talk to know what the other is thinking, Marty thought.

Annabelle went under the bed and retrieved the piss pot. She looked at the contents carefully.

"It is dark, there is blood in it."

"Have you passed stool?"

"What?" the count spat, grimacing from another spasm.

"Have you had a shit," Marty said in French.

"Yes, this morning."

Shelby gently palpated the area, took his pulse and looked in his eyes.

"I think you have bladder stones," he concluded, "and one is too big to pass. We need to take you to our surgery to perform an operation."

"Mon Dieu," the countess exclaimed.

"Do not worry we will not be cutting him open we will go in through—"

Marty stopped him, "Too much information, my friend. Let me reassure the countess while you two get the count dressed."

He escorted her outside. "He is in the best possible hands. I trust them with my own life and that of my family. Now let's get your coach around to the front."

Once at Shelby's house the count was taken into the surgery at the back. Marty and the countess waited and worried. Two hours later they emerged with a smiling count who was obviously not in pain but walked as if sore in the lower regions.

"We managed to find the stone and crush it," Shelby said. "He was able to pass it after that."

"How did you? Oh! Never mind." Marty realised he really didn't want to know.

"Ils ont mis un instrument dans ma piqûre," the count said.

That was too much information for Marty and he changed the subject.

"Can we take him home?"

"After tea," Annabelle said.

They sat and had an amicable high tea. The effect that Anabelle had on the household was evident everywhere from the decorations and furniture to the tea set that was used. The countess and Anabelle got on famously and looked to be becoming firm friends.

"Are you both going with Martin on his next mission?" the count asked.

"Yes, we will. Why?" Shelby replied.

"I am in need of a new doctor. It seems that the old fart that has been treating me is incompetent."

"Probably not incompetent, just out of date," Shelby said in the man's defence. "I can recommend a doctor who lives in Harley Street, which is not far from you. He is a modern physician who has been in practice for ten years or more."

Marty's next priority was to go and have a look at the Neaera and see how the modifications were progressing. She was at the dock in Blackwall and Angus met him at the gangplank.

"The work that required the drydock was completed a week ago. Her knees and ribs have been reinforced and the fitments for the guns added. The davits go on next, then we can bring the boats up."

"You have them already?"

"Yes, it's a new design." Angus led Marty to a stack of six boats on the dockside. "James helped design them with the master shipwright."

"They look like oversized punts."

"They are to some extent." The boats had a square prow like a punt that formed a ramp but much deeper sides and rowlocks for twelve men. Angus called a couple of men over and they turned it so it was the right way up.

"See here? The centre of the bench hinges up and out of the way allowing the marines to walk unhindered to the bow. There is room between the benches for them to stow their packs."

Marty climbed into the boat. He sat on a bench and bounced up and down to test its strength. Then he stood, lifting the centre section that was hinged beside where the oarsman would sit. It was cunningly fashioned with a centre support that hinged out of the way under gravity. The deck was boarded to make it smooth so the marines could easily walk to the prow.

"How does it handle at sea?"

"Surprisingly well, the men say fully loaded it is heavier than a longboat but not unmanageable."

"And in a swell?"

"Stable as it's got an almost flat bottom."

"How do you get the men off the beach?"

"Reverse procedure only we lay a gangplank from the bow for them to run up."

"Where is that stowed?" Marty said, looking around.

Angus grinned. "You are standing on it."

Marty looked down and realised the planking he was standing on was in fact a removable gangplank that could be slid forward over the bow.

Marty liked the ingenious design and sturdy build and was looking forward to seeing them in action. He clambered out and the men put it back on the stack.

"When do you get your guns?"

"Fletcher says they will be here at the end of the week. We have recalled the crew and they will start arriving later today."

"No uniforms."

"Aye, Sir, we got the message. Wolfgang passed it on."

The next visit was to Chatham. He met Wolfgang on the Unicorn which now had disguised gun ports and what looked like a shed on the fore deck. The disguise was very good. You would not see the concealed gun ports without a close inspection. The shed concealed their big fore deck carronades. Wolfgang had the gun crew show how it collapsed to the deck when they needed to go into action. Dummy crates covered the after carronades.

The top gallant and royal masts had been brought down, shortening them to more merchant-like heights. They could be raised at short notice if needed. Her hull had lost its Nelson pattern paint and was a uniform black. The gingerbread on her stern looked weather worn and slightly shabby. A look around the other ships showed they were equally well prepared.

"Good job, we sail in two weeks. I will come down with the Neaera."

Chapter 7: Reunion

Marty was in his study preparing to leave when there was a knock at the front door. He heard the mutter of voices as Adam answered it then there was a knock on his study door.

"Come in," Marty said, curious as to who it was.

Adam stepped inside and said, "You have a visitor, Milord, says he is an old friend."

He stepped aside and a man stepped through the door from behind him.

"Hello, Marty."

"Good God! Paul?"

There as large as life and twice as handsome was Paul La Pierre.

"I thought you were dead, man!" Marty cried and embraced his old friend.

"I nearly was," Paul said.

Marty looked at him. He had a rakish scar that ran up his cheek, across his forehead into his hair. When they shook hands, he saw he had a missing finger and the hand was scarred.

"Tell me what happened and where you have been." He looked at Adam. "Coffee please Adam."

They sat and Paul told his tale.

"When we made the raid on those ships, my charge went off prematurely. It was attached to the target, and we had started to move away but only got a few yards when it went up. The blast shattered the canoe, killed my man who was at the back and blew me into the water. I was unconscious as I must have hit something which opened me up." He pointed to the scar. "I also lost a finger, and my hand was damaged. It was fortunate that I must have been protected somewhat by Illingworth as he was directly between me and the charge."

Adam arrived with coffee. They took a sip and Paul continued.

"I was picked up by the Italian's guard boat and taken to a hospital. I was apparently unconscious for a month. When I did finally come around, I was as thin as a rake and couldn't remember anything."

"Nothing?" Marty said.

"Nothing. Not even my name. The Italians were very good to me. They let me wander around freely, gave me the name Marco Il Perduto and I learnt Italian."

"Mark the Lost," Marty translated. Paul nodded.

"I met a lovely girl called Margarita and we got married. I was having dreams of my past life that confirmed I had been a soldier but could only remember fragments. But I was happy living there, making a living from training horses. A skill I seemed to have from my past."

"You always were good with the nags."

"Well, all went well, and Margarita fell pregnant after three years and we had a son called Luca and a year after him a daughter called Isabella. She fell for a third, but she and the baby died in childbirth as he was breach."

"I am so sorry," Marty said.

"It is life. I was heartbroken but I had two young children to raise so I carried on."

"Did you remember anything?" Marty said

"Not much. Bits and pieces here and there. That is until I got thrown by a horse. A particularly vicious stallion owned by a local aristo that I was breaking. I landed on a railing and bashed my head again. I was knocked out and when I came around, I could remember everything."

"Strange thing the mind," Marty said.

"Well, the long and the short of it is, I had saved some money and was able to buy passage for me and the children to England. I went to my parents who were astonished to see me as they had been told I had been killed."

"I would think so! What did the marines say?"

"Well, they were sceptical that I was who I said I was to start with until I found one of my old officers who could identify me. You were away somewhere so I couldn't ask you."

"I was in India. What did they do?"

"They retired me, or rather, invalided me out. When I heard you were back in England I decided to come and see you."

"And very pleased I am, you did. Do you get a pension?"

"Yes, it is not much but as we live with my mother it is just enough."

Marty sat back and smiled.

"There is something you haven't remembered."

"What is that?"

"The social fund."

"The what? Oh! The social fund we all paid into. You are right, I had completely forgotten about it."

"Yes, you are entitled to a pension from that as well."

Marty went to his desk and took a piece of paper. "Let's see, you were wounded in 1809 that was eleven years ago. What was your pay then?"

"Ten bob a day."

He mumbled and muttered as he calculated and finally looked up and smiled, "You are due one thousand and three pounds, fifteen shillings in back pension and one hundred and eighty-two pounds a year from now on."

"Good grief that will make a difference."

"Aah but that doesn't stop there as there will be 5% interest on the back pay. I will have an accountant at the bank calculate it and send you what you are due. There is also your share of the prize money from that trip which would probably have been several thousand pounds as well. I will have the prize agent work it out and send you that as well."

Paul looked dumbfounded. "Marty, this is not why I came to see you."

"I know but it is what you are due." He stood and rang a bell. Adam arrived. "Have these notes delivered to Coutts and Miller the prize agent please, Adam."

"There that is the filthy mana taken care of. Come, you must see Caroline and twins."

"Where are Beth and James?"

"Beth is off on a mission. She lives here because it's in London and will be home sometime today. James is a midshipman on the Neaera, our new troop ship which is in Blackwall."

Caroline was in tears as she met Paul despite having been forewarned by Adam. She embraced him, much to his embarrassment and led him to a chair. He had to tell his story all over again. She asked about Margarita, and he produced a locket with her picture.

"She was very beautiful," she said.

Paul sighed and put the locket away.

"She was and I miss her dearly. Isabella is the image of her."

"You must bring them with you next time you visit."

"Where are you staying while you are in London?" Marty asked.

"I was going to go to the club."

"Nonsense," Carline said, and nodded at Adam.

Adam left the room and returned after a minute, "The blue room is being prepared, Milady."

"Thank you, Adam." She turned to Paul, "There, no excuses, you are staying here."

As they talked over the evening, they discovered the true extent of Paul's injuries. His back was scarred by burns. His left arm pierced through by a red-hot piece of iron which cauterised the wound but left him with a scar and stiffness. As a soldier he was finished. However, Marty had other ideas.

"You could still teach. You always were an excellent tactician, and your knowledge of guerrilla warfare is second to none."

"Who would have me? The marines won't."

"I would, if you would join us," Marty said.

"You are just being kind," Paul said sourly.

"Not at all. You know I do not carry passengers. You will earn your keep."

Paul knew that was true and gave himself a mental kick.

"Do you have a need then?"

"I do, as it happens, the SOF has been given a mission that includes training an army of rebels."

"I would gladly volunteer but what about my children?"

"They can come and live with us. The twins will go to school at Christchurch when the next school year begins, and the house will be empty of children. Mary and Tabetha will enjoy having little ones to look after and tutor. They are, what, seven and eight?"

"Yes, they are."

Paul thought for a few long moments. "Alright. I will do it."

Chapter 8: Shakedown

The trip down the Thames on the Neaera was regulation and they rendezvoused with the rest of the flotilla at the Roads. She sailed well even if she looked a little odd with the landing barges (as Marty thought of them) hanging from the davits.

Marty transferred to the Unicorn and gave the order to move all the extra marines from the flotilla ships to the Neaera. This was good practice for them as the barges were used and Marty insisted it was done with the same form as if they were landing.

The marines, with full packs and rifles, went over the side on cargo nets into the barges and took their seats. Their kit bags were loaded into the ship's boats and taken over separately. Then the loaded barges formed up and made for the Neaera as if they were returning from a landing. The troops disembarked and the barges returned to pick up the next lot. When the old hands saw Paul, a hullabaloo was sent up that could be heard around the harbour.

They set sail to gain the westing they needed to pass Ushant and the Bay of Biscay. As they were heading along the south coast of England Marty wanted them to stop at Sandbanks or Studland on the coast of Dorset to practise landing with the new barges. He also wanted to see them operate in open water.

They made landfall on the east beach of Studland Bay. This kept them out of the channel into Poole Harbour and, as the peninsula was uninhabited, a certain amount of privacy. The sight of fifty marines storming the beach might set off alarm bells across the county. However, the fishing fleet would be well aware that something was going on, but Marty wasn't worried about them. Fishermen had a habit of keeping their noses out of other people's business especially in an area renowned for smugglers.

The sea was running two-foot waves from the northeast and Marty ordered the flotilla hove to a half mile off the coast. There was a stiff north-easterly breeze pushing the waves along. The barges were lowered, and the men clambered down into them. They looked odd without uniforms and hats, but their composure and professionalism shone.

The boats on the lee side of the Neaera had an easy time of it as they were not moving around very much. On the windward side it was choppy, and the barges rolled. The marines soon discovered that in those conditions timing was everything. A couple got wet despite the efforts of the boat's crew and had to be fished out of the sea. Marty didn't mind as long as they didn't drown as it was all part of their training. Falling in got you a ribbing from your mates and sailors and marines seldom did it twice.

Loaded, the barges were heavier and more stable, but the twelve oarsmen had their work cut out to manoeuvre them into position. James was in the middle barge waving flags to get them into echelon formation. They took far too long to manage that and the landing on the beach was ragged.

They recovered to the Neaera and the oarsmen were rested and fed. In the afternoon they did it again. It was better but not perfect. They would overnight and try again in the morning.

James called the boat commanders together to analyse their performance. "I've called you together this evening to go over the landings," he said to the assembled coxes and marine commanders. "Suffolk, you are in the starboard end barge, what problems are you finding?"

"The effort the boys have to put in to get into position fair shags them out if they do start out on the windward side with a full barge. They are not easy to manoeuvre across the waves and roll something horrible with the waves on their beam."

"Do you have a suggestion?"

"If'n we could get all the boats around to the lee side before loadin' it would be better. We could walk them down the side of the ship and that would save the crew's strength."

"You others on the windward side agree?"

"Aye, Sir," said the other two coxes.

"Alright. Tomorrow, as soon as your oars are manned, you bring your barges astern of the ship in line astern. You wait until the first three are full and pull out towards the bow, then you follow them and take their places in turn."

James turned to Paul who was sitting with Declan O'Driscol, the captain of marines.

"Declan will be commanding the first wave. Can you command the second while they board?"

Paul nodded.

"Now let's talk about how we form up."

Marty and Angus were sipping port when James finished his debrief and entered the cabin. He looked at his father in surprise.

"I didn't know you were coming aboard," then remembering who his father was, added, "Sir."

Marty stood and ruffled his hair. Much to James's embarrassment. He poured them all a glass then asked, "How is Paul holding up?"

"Getting better every day. Tomorrow he will take command of the second wave."

Marty looked at him quizzically.

"The oarsmen on the windward side are wearing themselves out hauling the marines around to the leeward side. So, we will try a two-wave approach with the boats all being boarded from the leeward side."

"Good, do that and be ready to sail the morning day after tomorrow."

Marty stood. "I will send a boat into Poole tomorrow with mail. If you have letters to send, be ready at six bells of the afternoon watch." He said his goodbyes and had his barge take him back to the Unicorn.

That night James wrote letters to his mother, Beth and the twins and a long letter to Mellissa. He told her how much he missed her and how he thought about her all the time.

He was eighteen years old now and would sit his lieutenant's board after this trip. He was wondering whether to stay in the flotilla or look for another ship. He wasn't ambitious and was happy just to do his job. He liked command and the responsibility of caring for his men. He enjoyed a good fight and had more than his fair share of scars to prove his combat experience.

His letters finished, he went up on deck for some air. The moon was full, and the few clouds scudded across the sky. A set of white sails gleamed in the moonlight as a ship pulled into the Roads to anchor for the night not far from them. From the set of her sails, she was probably a frigate. He heard the splash of her anchor and the strains of a fiddler as they made her ready for the night.

A Shadow forewarned him that someone was approaching.

"Lovely night," Paul said.

"It certainly is."

"I never thought I would stand on the deck of a fighting ship ever again." Paul sighed.

"Father never thought he would see you again."

"Under normal circumstances I would have been exchanged and he would have known I was still alive. But they didn't know I was an officer. My tunic was lost, and we weren't carrying swords."

"From what he and Mother said, they both mourned your loss as a friend."

"I regret putting them through that."

"It's part of what we do. We make friends and they get killed or die of some exotic disease or just have an accident. We mourn them and move on," James said.

"That is very philosophical from a young man."

"I have seen and done a lot more than most midshipmen, but that goes for anybody in this flotilla."

"I have heard of some of your exploits."

"From the marines? Probably highly exaggerated then." James laughed.

"Your action in India seems to be legendary. You would have made a good officer of the marines."

"There was a time when I thought of moving over to them. But I love sailing too much."

"A sailor first and a fighter second, that makes sense. You don't want to follow your father in the other area?"

"No, Beth's the one who is into that side of things."

"Little Beth?"

"Not so little anymore. She is a demon with a sword, knife, and pistol. Can take most men in unarmed combat and loves the sneakiness."

"Killing doesn't bother her?"

"Not at all. She even studied anatomy, so she knows exactly where to hit for the best results."

"Lord, a chip of the old block."

"She is that."

The bell rang.

"That's me on watch. Talk to you later," James said.

The trials the next day went well. The new two-wave system suited the barges, and they could get all the men ashore in an acceptable time. It was adopted as their de facto method. That evening the crew and marines had a double ration of rum and there was dancing and singing on the deck. Marty listened as the sound drifted across the water, and smiled. Then he turned his attention to Captain Coats of the Frigate, Norwich, that had come aboard.

"The men on that brig are celebrating it seems," Coats said.

"Yes, they deserve to relax after a couple of hard days. Why did you wait for a day before reporting aboard?"

"I was told to meet a civilian convoy that would be anchored off off Poole. I recognised all your ships as being navy. I wanted to be sure before I acted."

Marty wondered how they knew he would stop here. Then realised Turner would have guessed he would shake down his new boats and Studland was the perfect place.

"Formerly navy, officially. Now owned by a private company."

"Including the Unicorn?"

"Absolutely."

He looked around at the crew who were obviously at navy rather than merchant strength and also knew that Marty and Wolfgang were still on the navy active list.

"Don't think about it too much," Marty advised. "Who ordered you to escort us?"

"Sir William," Coats said, referring to Sir William Johnstone Hope the First Sea Lord.

"Did he indeed?"

"I am to join the Ionian squadron."

"You will be based in Corfu?"

"Yes, but attached to an independent force."

Marty frowned. It sounded like he would be joining Leonidas and Nymphe. They didn't need an escort.

"Did he say anything else?"

Coats blushed. "He did say one thing. 'Tell Stockley that he better be back for the coronation', the bloody king is on my back about it. He was quite grumpy."

Marty burst out laughing.

Top masts were raised, and they sailed as soon as they could see a grey goose at a mile. Setting a course that would take them down the coast past Land's End and the Lizard out to the Scilly Isles and beyond. July was a good month for sailing as long as the Atlantic storms stayed away. Once they had gained enough westing to pass Ushant and the Bay of Biscay they turned south, the ships flying along under full sail. The Unicorn in the lead followed by the Endellion, then the Neaera and last the Eagle. The Norwich was a quarter mile off to windward.

"Twelve knots," Wolfgang reported.

"Clean bottoms work wonders," Marty said.

They both stood on the windward side of the quarterdeck content to let First Lieutenant, Gordon McGivern, sail the ship. Marty looked aft.

"The Neaera is a good sailor," he said.

"Angus is very happy with her," Wolfgang replied. "The marines like her as well."

"Yes, Declan said they had plenty of room to live in and store their equipment. She is a stable sailor as well."

"I heard they brought mortars."

"Yes, the Toolshed came up with a refined design of a four-inch tube mortar that is portable. They tested various designs of barrel until they came up with one that is both light and strong. One man can carry it on his back and another the mounting plate. Ingenious design, the barrel slots onto a ball brazed to the plate which stops it from sinking into the ground when it's fired. A pair of legs can be set to support the barrel at whatever angle you desire."

"Sounds like the barrel is quite long then."

"About two feet. The shell has a fuse that can be cut to length to detonate it at the required time and has a powder charge with a separate fuse fitted to the base. They light the propellant charge then drop the whole lot down the tube. Stand back and poof! The shell is launched with the shell's fuse lit by the propellant."

"How does one know how long to cut the shell's fuse?" Wolfgang asked.

"Oh, that's all taken care of. They have produced a manual with all the ranges, angles, times, and lengths. During a trial they dropped ten shells in a twenty-foot radius," Marty said proudly. "Declan has formed a new specialist platoon."

"Infantry born artillery, a real innovation."

They exercised the guns once a day to get the crews used to the new gunports and covers. Raised and lowered masts and generally honed the ship up to its usual high standard of efficiency. Marty noted that after watching them exercise for a day, the Norwich started her own exercises.

They entered the harbour at Gibraltar. Marty went to pay his respects to Commander in Chief of the Mediterranean fleet, Vice Admiral Graham Moore, on his flagship the one hundred- and twenty-gun Caledonia. It was quite a climb up the side of the huge ship's tumblehome to the entry port on the middle gun deck. Marty silently thanked the builder for his consideration. He was met by the flag captain and his first lieutenant who saluted smartly.

"Permission to come aboard," Marty said with a smile.

"Permission granted. Welcome aboard, Commodore," Captain Rutherford said even though Marty was dressed in civilian clothes. Marty shook their hands and said, "Is the admiral available?"

"Of course, please come with me."

He was led through the ship to the admiral's quarters and announced by the marine guard.

"Lord Martin, welcome. Thank You, Rutherford." Dismissed, the captain left.

"Sir Graham," Marty said as he shook hands.

"Please take a seat, can we offer you some refreshment?"

"Coffee, if you have it, thank you."

A steward went to brew up a pot and Sir Graham took up a letter checking it before looking directly at Marty.

"From First Sea Lord. Gives me very explicit and rather unusual instructions all to be held in the strictest confidence."

Marty waited.

"Am I allowed to know what you are up to?"

"As long as it stays here," Marty smiled.

"You have my word."

Marty explained the opportunity and what they needed to do to make it a reality.

"My god, you play for high stakes," Sir Graham exclaimed. "Cypress, along with Malta, would enable us to control the Middle East."

"Exactly."

"I have already ordered Leonidas and Nymphe to the Aegean. They will be joined by Norwich. They will use Corfu as their base of operations."

Norwich is there to keep an eye on us, Marty thought. Which in consideration wasn't a bad thing.

Sir Graham continued. "I have known Turner for many years. We were midshipmen together. I was surprised when he took over from Hood. Had no idea he was into all that skulduggery."

"Skulduggery that helped win the war," Marty said. Sir Graham nodded.

"I read the confidential files on what you did in Malta. Both times. Read like one of those modern thrillers. You have a reputation for being ruthless."

"When I have to be." Marty smiled.

Sir Graham shuddered. It was almost wolf-like.

There was a knock at the door and the steward brought in the coffee after which the conversation became more mundane around Marty's ships.

"That barque with the boats. What is she for?"

"Amphibious landings, the boats can get sixty marines ashore with full kit simultaneously."

"That must be useful for raiding."

"Absolutely. Get a force ashore, establish a beachhead then reinforce with a second wave. Usually at night or around dawn."

"Supported by your batteries. Must be very effective."

Marty was surprised Sir Graham had any kind of grasp of the concept. They got into a deep discussion about different landings they had been involved in. Then there was the sound of a signal cannon.

Sir Graham scowled. "Who the hell is making that damn noise?"

"Sorry, that's my captain. It's an hour until we sail, and he is recalling our shore teams. Which also means I must take my leave. With your permission?"

"Pfft, you don't need it. You and I answer to the same man," Sir Graham said, a little annoyed, then he softened. "I have the feeling you are going into a dangerous situation while the rest of us are languishing in peace. Take care, Stockley."

They sailed and Marty stood on the quarterdeck, Hector at his knee. The pup had been growing at a tremendous rate and ate accordingly. He had huge paws and the men all joked that he would grow into them and be a big dog. Marty found him as loyal, intelligent and protective as Blaez and Troy. Easy to train, he would do anything for a treat, and a confirmed lap dog. The latter characteristic would be a problem if he grew much bigger.

One thing he did that his father never did was sneak up onto Marty's cot at night. He would wake and find him lying tucked up against the back of his legs and once up would refuse to get down. One of the crew came to the steps and held up a tug toy he had made for Hector from a rope end that had a Turk's head knot tied in it. Marty sent Hector forward so he could be presented with it. A tug of war ensued that had the men cheering on the pup. Marty smiled indulgently and let the pup play on the main deck with the off-duty watch.

They passed through the straits of Heracles into the Mediterranean proper and set a course for Malta with all sails set. The weather was typical for the time of year. Men either tanned or burnt, leading to a constant stream of men heading to the sick bay where they were treated with Aloe Vera. Marty took the opportunity to get rid of his officer's arms (a tan that only covered his forearms) by going shirtless. The men joked you could see him changing colour. He tanned so fast.

Chapter 9: Malta

They sailed into Valletta harbour and as they were supposed to be merchantmen, didn't salute the flag. It felt very strange as Marty's boat took him ashore. The boys spread out to keep an eye on him as he made the short walk to the Governor's Palace with Hector at his side. His briefing notes said that the governor had been informed of his mission and to coordinate with him.

Sir Thomas Maitland, grey haired, high forehead and thin of face, met Marty in his office. He came around the desk and greeted him.

"Viscount Stockley, how are you?"

"Good afternoon, Sir Thomas, I am very well, thank you. I hope I find you hearty and well?"

"I am in excellent health. Malta suits me. What are you up to this time?"

Marty grinned and took a chair, Hector plonked himself down at his feet. He waited until coffee had been served and the servant departed before answering.

"Greece is bubbling up to explode into open rebellion against their Ottoman masters."

"Yes, I know. They have already tried and failed once."

"Indeed, and that is why I am going there with my little flotilla as a private individual. To train them and guide them to success."

"I suspected as much from the cryptic message from London. There was a hint of a big prize for us if they gained independence."

"Cyprus."

"What? The whole island?"

"Yes."

"But that would change the whole power map of the eastern Mediterranean."

"It would and will change the Middle East forever."

"Well, anything I can do to help is yours for the asking."

"Thank you. How has the island been since my last visit?"

"Quieter, and more lawful. Even the Cartel are behaving themselves and keeping things within bounds. We reformed the police force along British lines, strengthened it and made Captain Falzon the commander."

"I should say hello while I am here."

"That's easy, the police headquarters is just across the square."

"I will route all my messages back to Britain through you if that is acceptable."

"Of course, is there anything else?"

"Not at the moment."

Marty stood to leave. Sir Thomas escorted him to the door.

The police headquarters was, on the surface, quiet. He introduced himself at the desk and asked to see Captain Falzon. He only had to while away a couple of minutes watching the smartly-uniformed policemen coming and going before Falzon himself came to fetch him.

"Martin, hello! I didn't see any warships in port."

"That's because we snuck in under false colours," Marty grinned.

Falzon's office was on the top floor, and he could see the harbour over the rooftops.

"Your dog?"

"Yes, he is just a pup, three months old."

"Lord, he is going to be big!"

Marty patted Hector on the head, and the pup climbed up on his lap.

"That is going to be a problem when he is full grown." Mateus laughed.

"The governor told me you are the new police chief."

"Yes, he reformed the militia I led before, in the way the British force is modelled. We now have constables, sergeants and inspectors."

"Enough to keep the Cartel under control?" Marty asked, referring to the main criminal organisation on the island.

"The first thing we did was limit the number of brothels and closed down all the opium dens."

"I bet they didn't like that."

"No, I had a visit from Mr Tanti almost immediately. He was very angry until I pointed out that all I had to do was ask, and you would come back. After that he was a real charmer."

"Well, I will be in the area for months so that isn't so unrealistic."

"I won't ask what you are up to."

Marty smiled.

As the ships were reprovisioning Marty, Shelby and Annabelle took the opportunity to visit the theatre to see a comic opera by Françoise-Adrien Boieldieu. Jean de Paris was a tale about the prospective marriage of the Princess of Navarre, to the Dauphin. The lead Soprano was someone they all knew. Veronica Southerland was still on the island.

"Marty!" Veronica squealed as she joined them in the bar after the performance.

"Still using the opera as a cover, I see," Marty said as she hugged him.

"It's the other thing I am good at," she smiled. "But I am only the understudy. This was my last performance as the prima donna comes back to the island tomorrow after a holiday in Italy.

"You and I need to talk," Marty said.

"I know, I got a message from my new boss."

"Good, so I don't have to rush then."

They enjoyed a drink and Marty invited her to visit him on the Unicorn in the morning.

The next morning Marty had a boat waiting for Veronica at the dock. She arrived, to the delight of the sailors, dressed in a summery dress and fancy hat that only an actress would wear. She was hoisted aboard on a chair and several men rushed forward to help her down until Billy stepped forward and held out his hand.

"Hello, Billy," she smiled, a softness in her eyes.

"Hello, Miss Veronica, I'm very pleased to see you."

"Is it me or has Billy scrubbed himself up?" Wolfgang said to Marty.

"I believe he has. I didn't think he had any feelings for her last time we were here."

"Well from what I can see the feelings, if there are any, are absolutely mutual." Wolfgang grinned as the two stood looking into each other's eyes.

"Well, I'm damned," Marty said.

Veronica suddenly realised they were being watched by the entire crew and Marty and Wolfgang who were standing patiently waiting for her. She blushed and said something to Billy before moving to the quarterdeck.

After she left, Matai stepped up beside Billy and nudged him with his elbow. "You old dog." Billy looked bashful and shuffled his feet to the gentle ribbing of his crewmates.

Marty, Wolfgang and Veronica settled down in Marty's cabin while Adam served coffee and tea. They forwent teasing her about Billy.

"Did the admiral tell you what we are going to be doing?"

"Only that you will be operating in the Aegean, and from that I assume it's something to do with the deal you did with the Filiki Eteria."

"Well deduced, that is exactly the reason. We need to live up to my promises so we can take control of Cyprus."

"What do you need from me?"

"The admiral told me you had been trained as a controller."

"Yes, I run the agents here, Sicily and the Ionian Islands."

"Well now I want you to expand your network in Greece. The Ionian Islands are a British Protectorate under the control of the governor, so you can set up an office there."

Veronica looked thoughtful for a long moment.

"I have a very good agent on Kefalonia, but I need someone who can operate as my messenger and guard who I can trust explicitly."

Marty looked at Wolfgang and winked. "I think we know someone who has extensive experience of assisting a controller."

Wolfgang, with a completely straight face, said, "He was much younger then, of course."

"But he was very effective and not afraid to do some of the dirty work," Marty said. "Francis spoke very highly of him."

"You have someone who worked for Francis Ridgley?" Veronica said enthusiastically.

"He did. Francis trained him himself."

"Can I meet him?"

"I will have him brought in." Marty nodded to Adam who knew exactly who they were talking about.

A few moments later there was a knock on the door and Marty called, "Enter."

Billy stepped through. "You wanted to see me, Milord?"

"I have a job for you. Veronica needs someone to act as her go between to her agent on Kefalonia and help her set up an operations room and as you worked with Francis, you are the ideal man."

Veronica looked delighted and Billy was trying very hard to suppress a grin.

"When do I start?"

"Now is as good a time as any. Sit down and you can get acquainted," Marty said.

A snort of a laugh was heard from the steward's galley.

"The first thing I want to do is make contact with Georges Hondras, if he is still here," Marty continued ignoring the interruption.

"He is. I will contact him this afternoon."

"Arrange for us to have dinner tomorrow. Choose a quiet but good restaurant where we can talk privately."

"I will send you a message with Billy when it is arranged."

"Good, after we have talked with him, we can work out the next steps."

Billy moved ashore, straight into Veronica's apartment. Marty didn't care if the two wanted to nest, that was fine by him, as long as they did their job. Marty wrote a report for Turner and encoded it before sending it on a passing warship that was on its way home.

Billy arrived with word that Georges was happy to talk to Marty and they should meet for dinner at Zizka in West Street at 6 pm the following day.

Georges was already waiting when Marty arrived. Marty noted the absence of any guards and signalled for his escort to fall back.

"Kalosorises xana, Martin, welcome back." Georges held out his hand.

"Nice to see you again too," Marty smiled and shook it.

"The weapons and gold have been delivered as you promised. We thank you for that," Georges said with a bow of his head.

"It's time for us to live up to the rest of my promises," Marty said, "I have a contingent of trainers and advisors to help build your army."

Georges grinned happily. "That, my friend, is very good news. You heard that the fools in the north launched an attempt with just an untrained militia?"

"Yes, I did, and it failed."

"Not only did they fail, but a lot of good people were killed. The Ottomans' reprisals extended as far as executing the families of the rebels."

"A lesson learnt. Empty gestures cost. If you are going to fight, be sure you can win."

"We have the men, they need training and we need guidance on the battlefield."

"I need to know where to send my ships and have someone tell the Filiki that we are coming."

"I can help with both. We have men in the Peloponnese and there are several islands that are ripe to rebel."

"Anywhere in the north?"

"Yes, to the north of the Gulf of Corinth, but the south is the most important as the capital is there. If we can control that we can claim independence."

"We have enough men to train both, and officers who can be on hand to advise."

"Let me go and see where we need them, and I will get back to you. It will take me seven days. I will leave tomorrow."

"Would it speed things up if I move my ships to the Ionian Islands?"

"That would save two days. Where will you be?"

"I don't know the islands. Where would you suggest?"

"Zakynthos would be best, I think. On the east coast there is Zakynthos harbour that is deep enough for your ships. I will meet you there in five days."

They ate their meal, and the subject of Egypt came up.

"They never did gain independence and are still under the Ottomans thumb," Georges said with a shrug.

"It will come. Their revolt inspired other countries to think of independence as well. Their biggest problem was a lack of allies amongst the large powers. The Russians wouldn't back them as they are Muslim, the British don't want to be seen to go overtly against the Ottomans, the French are busy helping them build a canal, and don't want to rock the boat by sending military assistance."

"At least we have your assistance and the Russians."

"I wish it could be more overt, but it is what it is." Marty sighed.

Chapter 10: Zakynthos

The flotilla arrived in the harbour of Zakynthos, which to Marty's eye was ideal. Sheltered, deep with good holding ground and the capital of the island. The island was under British protection, and the British flag flew over the town.

Veronica and Billy had come along, and Marty gave her the bad news.

"I would like it if Billy could set up shop here with your local agent. That way he can send you reports, and you can send him instructions for your people."

Veronica looked him in the eye. "I disagree."

"You do?"

"Yes, and before you say anything it has got nothing to do with what we feel for each other."

Marty crossed his arms and waited for her to continue.

"Billy needs training, and I cannot do that with him here and me in Malta. In any case I think that we both need to be here on the island. He can be my protector and I can build a new network from here across Greece."

Marty couldn't fault her logic. It was what he thought as well, but he wanted her to put it forward.

"Alright, we will do it like that. Get ashore and find yourself a place to rent. Billy can give you some advice about setting up an operations room."

Billy remembered Francis's cork-lined garret in Gibraltar with mixed emotions. It had been a refuge and the place where he learnt about interrogation and murder.

Veronica and Billy walked from the docks after the Unicorn's jolly boat brought them ashore. They wandered into town looking for empty apartments or houses. Veronica spoke Greek and talked to a shopkeeper.

"He says we should ask at the town hall," Veronica said after the man had spoken to her slowly and carefully.

"Why was he talking to you like you were an idiot?"

"Because I only know classical Greek, not the dialect they use here. He had to talk slowly so I could understand him."

They found the town hall which was back at the docks and entered. There was the usual desk, and she went through the routine of telling the clerk what she wanted. He looked them over, then said in good English, "Your Greek is good if a little stilted, it would be better if you adapted to the local dialect if you are going to live here."

Veronica had to work hard to keep her annoyance with the pretentious prick from showing.

"As to a house to rent, I do know of a couple of empty ones which the owners may rent out. Do you have furniture?"

"No, we don't," Billy said.

"I can show you where to buy that as well. Now let's talk about my fee."

Billy bristled, thinking they were about to be fleeced. Veronica put a restraining hand on his arm.

"What are you asking for?" she said in the sweetest of voices.

"Twenty percent of the rental for six months and fifteen percent of the cost of the furniture. You do know what percent means?"

She ignored the insult.

"That's extortionate. We will pay ten percent of four month's rent and five percent of the cost of the furniture."

"Madam, that wouldn't get me out from behind this desk. Fifteen percent of six month's rent and ten percent of the furniture."

"My final offer. Fifteen percent of four month's rent and seven percent of the furniture."

The man looked at her sourly. "Agreed. You have done this before."

"We came from Malta," she replied and he nodded knowingly as the Maltese were renowned for their shrewd bargaining. He stood and led them outside, locking the door.

"Are you the mayor?" Billy asked.

"No, that lazy bastard is at home sleeping off lunch. I am his clerk. I do all the work. My name is Tassos."

Tassos took them to a three-storey house two hundred yards from the docks that fronted onto a market square. Stalls were set up and a huge variety of vegetables and meat (alive and dead) were on sale.

"There is a fish market near the southern dock where the boats come in," Tassos informed them. "This is just a small market that is here three days a week."

He looked around and walked over to a bar where a group of men were drinking ouzo and smoking pipes. He returned with a large man with an impressive moustache.

"This is Santos, the house was his mother's. He wants to know how long you want to rent it for?"

"A year," Veronica said. "Maybe longer."

Tassos gave her a look out of the corner of his eye. She smiled sweetly at him.

"He says you can have it for one hundred drachma a month."

Veronica switched to Greek.

"I will pay fifty and give you six months in advance in silver." She held her hand out to shake on the deal.

That caught both men by surprise and Santos took her hand automatically.

"Good, we have an agreement." She nudged Billy who took out a purse, coincidently showing the pistol he had on his left hip butt forward. Six months' rent was counted out and handed over.

Tassos growled something to Santos who shrugged and handed her a key. He went back to his friends.

Veronica handed over Tassos's commission.

"You are a witch and will be burnt after he tells everyone how you duped him," Tassos grinned.

"He won't," Veronica replied confidently, "he is too proud."

They went inside and found it to be roomy and relatively clean if bare of furniture. Veronica made notes on every room after she had Billy pace them out. Then they went furniture shopping.

The bed was delivered that same day, so they moved in and a wonderfully, not so, peaceful night was had by both of them where the strength of the bed was thoroughly tested.

Marty visited as soon as they sent him the address. He arrived as the majority of their furniture was being delivered. He dodged into the house around a sofa being carried by two delivery men.

"Morning, Boss," Billy said cheerfully as he carried a basket of crockery into the living area.

"Good morning, Billy. Busy I see."

"I got something to show you." Billy grinned as he put the basket on a table. He led Marty further into the house and up a flight of stairs to the third floor.

"The old lady who lived here had some secrets." Billy went to the end of the hall and stood facing a seemingly blank wall. Marty followed curiously.

Billy pressed the toe of his boot against the board that ran around the wall at floor level. A section moved inwards and there was a click. He pushed the wall and a hidden door opened. Inside was a fully-furnished boudoir with erotic paintings, a chair with straps that could be used to restrain a person in various positions and a large bed.

Marty walked over to what would be an umbrella stand in another room and saw it contained a number of canes, horse whips, and paddles. There was a bridle hung above it whose straps were definitely not meant for a horse.

"Looks like the old girl had a line of business going," Billy said.

Marty nodded and ran a hand over the wall.

"Cork lined; this room must be pretty soundproof."

"That's what I thought. Perfect innit? For an operations room, I mean."

Marty nodded.

"Be discreet when you get rid of this stuff. You don't want to embarrass your landlord as he obviously doesn't know this room exists or he would have cleared it," Marty said.

"Aye, aye, Boss. Don't want to tip him off that there was another room either as he will put up the rent."

"How did you find it?"

"I noticed we are a room short on this floor and started looking. Then figured the corridor was too short, so started pressing things and there it was."

"Good job."

Billy smiled at the praise.

Veronica found them; her face was dirt smudged and her hair tied up in a scarf.

"Hello, Milord Martin," she said.

"Just Martin or preferably Marty, we don't need to give people hints to who I am."

"Alright," she smiled.

"This will make a good operations room once you clear out the furniture and equipment."

Veronica grinned and indicated the chair. "We will keep that to use during interrogations."

Marty could see the sense in that and joked, "As long as that's all it gets used for."

His local team set up and running, Marty turned his attention to the mainland. He called his captains together.

"We can expect Georges any day now, so get your ships watered and provisioned ready to move at short notice. Wolfgang, I want a crew for one of those larger fishing boats put together under Midshipman Donaldson to act as a messenger. Fletcher is acquiring one from a boatbuilder on the edge of the town. We were told he has one on stock that was built without a buyer as they always need replacements."

"Five men plus a master's mate to cox her should be sufficient for one of those," Wolfgang said.

"I agree," Marty said.

"Should we have the carpenters look it over?"

"Wouldn't do any harm, but no modifications, it is to stay a fishing boat."

"Understood, Sir."

Fletcher returned later that afternoon. He looked grumpy.

"Something wrong?" Wolfgang asked.

"I think I have been fleeced."

"How so?"

"I paid for a ship ready to sail."

"What's missing?"

"Sails."

"No sails?"

"The boatyard say that sails are the responsibility of the owner."

"Aah."

"They didn't mention that until the boys arrived to sail her around."

"What did they do?"

"Rowed it. They said they would make sails when they got here."

"Then what's the problem?" Wolfgang asked, puzzled.

"I paid the price I thought fair for a fully-equipped boat."

"How much less would you have paid if you had known?"

"The cost of the canvas at least!" Fletcher harrumphed.

"How much would that be for a boat that size?" Wolfgang said.

"About ten bob."

"What did the boat cost?"

"The equivalent of twelve quid."

Wolfgang shook his head. "That's not a big difference."

"It's the principle!" Fletcher said and stomped off.

"What was that about?" First Lieutenant Gordon McGivern said as he joined Wolfgang.

"Less than a shilling in the pound," Wolfgang said. "Pursers, I will never understand them, you would think it's their money they are spending."

Veronica had contacted her agent in the Ionian Islands who was based on Corfu a half day's sail away. By the time he arrived they had the house straight.

Kostas was a rogue. He made no apologies or excuses for it. He swindled, stole, smuggled, and was a notorious womaniser. He had his own ship, an ancient-looking polacre called the σειρήνα (siren). Looks were deceiving, there was nothing old or shabby about the ship's rigging or running gear once you wiped away the tar. The hull was as solid as a rock. His one redeeming quality was he hated the Ottomans with a passion and by working with the British he got to hurt them almost every day.

He was a good-looking man who strutted rather than walked, shoulders back and head held high. His clothes were worn but well-made and fitted to show off his muscular physique. He saw Veronica sat in the café he had agreed to meet her at, and prepared to make his entrance. He scowled as he saw a big man of similar age to her sit at the table with glasses of wine. From the looks between them they were a couple.

He recovered his swagger as he thought, *she will still find me irresistible.* How wrong could he be.

Billy had seen Kostas enter the square, pause and the look on his face as he saw that Veronica was not alone. He had him pegged for what he was immediately.

"Your strutting peacock is here."

Veronica looked around and saw Kostas.

"He does, doesn't he."

Kostas reached their table and bowed dramatically over her hand. Billy just watched. A neutral expression on his face.

"Kostas, sit down. We have work to do," Veronica said in Greek. "This is Billy, he is working with me."

He looked slightly put out that she didn't give him a gushy greeting.

"What is happening?" he said.

"You saw the four ships in the harbour?"

He nodded.

"They are going to Greece and the islands to train the men for the rebellion."

"They have the men?"

Just then a roar of laughter came from another table.

"Look around, this bar is full of them."

Billy whistled and every face turned towards them. He lent forward and the butt of his pistol showed.

"Every one of them," Billy said in a soft, dangerous voice.

Kostas looked uncomfortable so Billy whistled again, and the men went back to their drinks and conversations.

"We need to find any informants or sympathisers who are hiding in the rebel forces. Do you have men you can trust on the mainland?" Veronica said.

Now Kostas was all business.

"I have been working with several across the peninsula and around the gulf, all men I would trust with my life."

"Are any part of the rebel movement?"

"They all are in some way."

"Good." Veronica looked up and smiled. "I want you to meet someone."

Kostas looked around and saw a man dressed in a long coat with an open-necked shirt underneath. His tight trousers were tucked into high-legged boots. His hair was pulled back and tied.

The man kissed Veronica's hand and nodded to Billy before pulling up a chair.

"This is Martin, he is my superior," she said.

Martin nodded in greeting and said something in English to Veronica. She replied and he smiled then turned to Kostas. A gold coin appeared in his hand as if from nowhere held between two fingers. Veronica translated for him.

"Martin wants you to watch the collaborators and find out who they report to. Then follow that person and find out who he reports to and so forth until you find out who the Ottoman head of intelligence is. He will pay you twenty of these gold pieces once he has the name and location of all the people."

Marty flipped the coin to Kostas who plucked it out of the air and bit it. It was a golden guinea but that didn't matter. Gold was gold.

"We already know who the informants are and were going to kill them," Kostas said.

"Do not do that as it will alert the Ottomans that something is going on. We need to find out who is running the network so we can feed him false information," Marty said.

"Alright we will do as you say. Where do I find you?"

"You don't. You will report to Veronica and she will get messages to me, and don't be surprised if the rebels start to disappear. We will be training them."

Georges arrived and left with Marty and the flotilla. They were to meet the men in charge of the rebellion. Georges told him, "There are five men who we will meet. Generals Theodorus Kolokotronis, Ogysseas Androutsos, and Dimitris Plapoutas, Pastor Papaflessass, and Bishop Germanos of Patras. These are the force behind the revolution.

The two clergymen, Papaflessass and Germanos are politicos and diplomats, but you will see Papaflessas fighting alongside the men as well. He is a firebrand and can motivate the peasants; he is also tight with the Russians."

"What about the others?"

"Military men. General Kolokotronis is the most senior. Androutsos is the head of the eastern mainland and a warrior. General Plapoutas went to the Ionian Islands during 1811 and was an officer in the 1st Regiment Greek Light Infantry."

"They are not short of military experience, why are they so keen for us to train their men?"

"Because you know modern techniques and tactics. The British army is famous after Waterloo, and they admire them. Especially the Rifles. General Kolokotronis has managed to form a confederation of the Moreot irregular Klepht bands. They are a bunch of highwaymen turned rebels. He needs them made into a modern army."

"How long have we got?"

"They have tentatively set June as the start of the insurrection."

"Ten months. Long enough," Marty said thoughtfully.

Chapter 11: Mainland Greece

The ships slipped into the Gulf of Argolic to the village of Paralio Astros and anchored a safe distance from the shore. Marty and Georges went ashore and made their way to the village of Astros and the church of St. Anargyron. They walked into the cool dim nave and were met by a bearded man dressed in the black of the Greek orthodox clergy.

"Your Eminence," Georges said, hands cupped right over left in front of him. "Lord Martin, may I introduce his Eminence, Bishop Germanos. Your Eminence, this is Viscount Stockley of British Intelligence."

"I know of you, Lord Stockley. My brothers in the Feliki Etera have talked of how you have helped us." His English was good.

"Your Eminence, I am pleased to meet you," Marty said with a bow.

"Come, we will meet with the others in the vestry." He led them through the church to a door that led out of the nave by the elaborate altar. Inside was a spacious room with a table and chairs and a rack of vestments. The bishop introduced him to the four personages sat at the table who stood as they entered.

Marty greeted each in turn, the military men dressed in traditional Greek clothes rather than uniform and the cleric Papaflessas dressed in a faded red robe and hat. Marty noted that the main difference between the military and church was the amount of facial hair. The churchmen had full beards of impressive length while the soldiers sported handlebar moustaches.

General Kolokotronis opened in Greek which Georges translated. "Georges tells us that you have come with weapons and men to train us."

"I have a cargo of muskets, ball and powder and eighty marines to train your armies."

"That is more than enough men. What will you do with so many?"

"I plan to divide them into four. Twenty of my men can train an army of a thousand men. You have many men dispersed in different locations, here on the peninsula, the mainland, and the islands. Where you don't have leaders with military experience, I have officers who can advise them in both battlefield and guerrilla tactics."

"What experience do you have?"

"Me? I am a navy man. However, I was at Waterloo with Wellington and have fought with the Rifles. I have also fought on land in Italy and South America."

"Why don't you wear a uniform?" Papaflessas said.

"The British government wishes to keep our involvement covert. I hold the rank of Commodore in the Royal Navy and the flotilla are all former navy ships that are now privately owned."

"So, you are a spy?" Papaflessas said, a hint of scorn creeping into his voice.

Marty smiled at him. "I am a senior agent. It is true I occasionally get asked to find out things the enemies of my nation wish to keep secret." Marty had decided that with these men honesty was the best policy.

"So as an ally we are quite safe?" Papaflessas said unconvinced.

"As safe as you are with the Russians." Marty smiled.

The bishop stepped in. "I am sure Lord Martin and his government are acting with good faith." Marty bowed his head in acknowledgement. "Papaflessas has strong ties to the Russian church."

"I'm not here to interfere with that. Just to fulfil my end of the bargain I made with the Feliki Etera," Marty said.

"When can you bring your men ashore?" General Kolokotronis said.

"Anytime, we can go down to the beach and watch them come ashore now if you like. We plan to do it as a practice landing."

"That I would like to see," Plapoutas said.

"Do you have an army here?" Marty asked.

"Yes, we have another north of the Gulf of Corinth, and the important island is Crete."

"What about Rhodes?"

"Rhodes will not rebel. They are too close to the Turkish mainland. That is not to say that they will not help. There are many members of the Filiki Eteria on the island and I am sure they will go to the aid of the rebellion when it starts."

Georges told Marty later that there were a number of rebel armies scattered around the peninsula, but Kolokotronis's was the biggest.

The group walked from the village back to the beach opposite to where the ships were moored. The Neaera was closest to shore less than a half mile off. Marty spotted a glint from a telescope lens on the quarterdeck of the Neaera followed by more glints from the other ships. Confident he was being closely watched he used his arms to semaphore a brief message. The Neaera's flag dipped in acknowledgement.

"What did you tell them?" General Plapoutas asked.

"To send twenty-five men and an officer." Marty had his watch in his hand.

The Greeks exchanged looks when whistles sounded across the water. The three barges on the landward side of the ship were lowered. Marty was proud they did it in synchronisation. As soon as the boats hit the water the oarsmen shinnied down the ropes and took up their stations along with their cox. Nets were lowered over the side and marines in red uniforms climbed down into the boats. Which, as soon as they were full, formed into a line and headed for the beach.

The three barges came up onto the sand together and the marines debarked over the bow and formed up in two lines with Declan O'Driscol at the fore.

"Fourteen and a half minutes from acknowledgement to the last man on the beach," Marty said to Declan. "Well done."

The Greeks had followed him forward and were looking at the marine's uniforms.

"There are no insignia," General Plapoutas noted.

"No, nor are the uniforms those of the marines."

"They carry muskets, not rifles."

"The same ones we have brought for your men. Which are being unloaded now."

Nets of crates were being offloaded into the barges which had returned to the Neaera.

"You had better organise some transport," Marty said.

General Kolokotronis barked an order to some men who had appeared at the top of the beach.

Not as relaxed as you would have me believe; Marty smiled inwardly as he saw they were soldiers. Then scanned the dunes for his own men. He spotted Chin who, once he saw him, disappeared.

In an hour there were men with hand and donkey carts lined up to take the crates of guns, casks of ball and powder away. Marty was about to give instructions to Declan when Antton and Garai appeared dragging someone between them.

"What is this?" General Kolokotronis said.

"Who are these men?" Papaflessas said.

"They are my men. They have been guarding the landing and making sure we weren't being observed."

"Found this one watching the beach. He was hiding in the scrub at the back," Antton said.

"Is he one of your men?" Marty asked Kolokotronis.

"I do not think so."

"Georges, I want to question him. Would you be so kind as to translate?"

"Of course."

"We will have to probably beat any information out of him."

The man started and looked at Marty with fear in his eyes."

"Now that is interesting, you understand English," Marty said.

The man gabled in Greek.

"Is it me, or is his accent off?" Marty said to Georges.

"You have a good ear. Yes, his accent has a trace of Macedonian."

Marty stepped up close and said softly in his ear, "I know you understand me. I am going to cut strips of your flesh away and feed them to my dog until you tell me everything. Then I will burn your body so you cannot go to heaven. If you tell me what I want to know I will give you an honourable death."

The man was shaking. The coldness of Marty's tone and the way he spoke of mutilation and pain chilled him to the bone. It didn't help when Marty's barge pulled up on the beach and Hector bounded over. He decided he didn't like the man and sat on Marty's left growling.

It was pure coincidence that Marty had arranged for his barge to arrive once the offloading had been completed. Hector had decided he had had enough of being separated from his boss and jumped in before it left. It didn't matter as the result was that the man started to talk.

Several days later Marty hosted the Greek generals in his cabin. Declan and his men had started training the army in its encampment which was some twenty-five miles away at Valtetsi.

"The man my men captured is a Muslim who works for the Ottomans. He has been observing your goings on for several weeks and reporting them to his contact in Corinth through a chain of couriers."

"Have you killed him?" Kolokotronis said.

"No. We will use him to feed false information to the Ottomans."

"How will you know he is doing what you tell him to?"

"Because we have tested him already. We had him write a message and encode it. It is a simple cypher that any moderately-educated man can use. We also searched his house and found a code book in the form of a scroll, and a cache of Ottoman gold coins."

"Did you torture him?"

"Only by putting him in a very uncomfortable position and denying him sleep. He is not a strong man but is very religious. The threat of being denied access to heaven was enough with the other measures."

"What do you intend to do next?" Plapoutas said.

"The secret to counterespionage is to keep the flow of information running with real but insignificant information and to inject a misdirection at a key moment," Marty said.

"Will you stay here and oversee that?" Kolokotronis said.

"I won't but the man in charge of the marines will. I also have people who are mapping the Ottoman's intelligence network. My role is to set up the infrastructure and put the right people in the right places."

"The men that captured the informer on the beach. Who are they?" Androutsos said.

"My team. They are called the Shadows."

"We only saw two, how many are there?"

"There are seven, but one is also my cook. Six of them were on the beach and providing security during our meeting."

"We never saw them."

"There was one on a rooftop near the church covering the entrances with a rifle." At that moment Adam walked in with some freshly-made cakes. "And here he is. Adam is a crack shot and can take the centre out of a playing card at two hundred and fifty yards."

Adam sketched a bow.

"Four were outside the church and one inside."

"Inside?" Kolokotronis said.

"Yes, he was posing as a worshipper."

Georges was grinning as he translated. The Greeks exchanged looks.

Androutsos broke the silence. "I need to get back to my men in the east."

"We can take you. We will move the flotilla into the Aegean under the Greek flag to intercept any Ottoman ships after we drop you and the marines off."

The meeting broke up. Androutsos stayed and sent a message with the others for his baggage to be sent from the camp along with his batman. Marty would divide his cabin to accommodate him.

Androutsos turned out to be a gracious guest. He was trying to learn English and Georges would spend all his free time teaching him. Marty liked his bluff, honest, simple approach to life. Marty took him on a tour of the Unicorn while they waited for his things.

"The main guns are eighteen pounders; the men can fire two broadsides every two and a half minutes." They toured through the ship and back up to the main deck where Shelby and Annabelle were taking the air.

"Let me introduce you to our physicians. Mr and Mrs Shelby."

The general was surprised if not shocked to see a woman, and such a beautiful woman as her, on a ship of war.

"Seeing me on deck helps convince observers that this is a merchantman," Annabelle said, seeing the look on his face.

"You are both physicians?"

"Yes, we are," Shelby said with a hint of warning in his voice. He was very protective of Annabelle.

"I meant no offence, but it is unheard of in Greece for a woman to be in medicine unless she is a local healer."

By healer they assumed he meant herbalist.

"Then you are wasting a lot of talent," Shelby said.

The general's luggage was delivered along with his batman. An evil-looking, little man who carried a wicked-looking curved knife. He was reputed to be fiercely loyal to the general and was never far from his side once he boarded.

The ships set sail with the wind from the north. They exited the gulf turning northeast to head towards the strait of Keas and on to the strait between the southern end of the Ottoman-controlled island of Eğriboz (Euboea) and the northern end of the island of Andros. From there they would tack to the north-northwest and sail up the east coast of Eğriboz to its northern tip, staying as close to the wind as they could. Finally, they would turn southwest to enter the Gulf of Malian and the fishing village of Kamena.

The ships formed up, with the Unicorn and Neaera in line astern a cable apart with the Eagle and Endellion ranging out ahead to either side. They would take no chances with the general.

They were about to pass between Eğriboz and Skyros when the Eagle out ahead to the east fired a gun and made a signal.

"Eagle has signalled – strange sail in sight," Midshipman Browning reported.

Wolfgang sent a messenger down to inform Marty. He wasn't concerned as that part of the Aegean was a regular route for commerce.

"Commodore says to keep him informed," Midshipman Donaldson said, returning to the deck with alacrity.

Wolfgang nodded and scanned the horizon ahead with his telescope.

Another cannon fired, this time from behind them.

"Neaera signalling, strange sail aft."

Wolfgang frowned. He looked to the Endellion and focussed his glass.

A signal shot up and there was the puff of smoke as a gun fired on her port quarter.

"Signal from Endellion Sir. Enemy in sight," Midshipman Browning squeaked in excitement.

"Steady, boy, they are a way off yet," Gordon McGivern said.

Marty had heard the cannon and came up on deck followed by the general.

"What is it?" Marty asked Wolfgang.

"A trap. One from the east, one from the west and one from behind," Wolfgang said.

"Interesting. Now how did they know we would be here?"

The general spoke in rapid Greek.

"The general wants to know what is going on," Georges said.

"Our Ottoman friends are trying to intercept us. My guess is they are expecting us to be merchantmen. We will let them come and give them a warm greeting."

Wolfgang knew what to do, they had done this many times.

"Bring us to quarters, Gordon. Keep everything covered and the men out of sight."

"Aye, aye, Sir."

Gordon bellowed orders and the crew moved into the ballet they had rehearsed so many times. The general watched with interest and Georges pointed out that the Neaera was also preparing.

"Signal the schooners – plan D," Marty said.

"What does that mean?" the general said.

"The schooners will stay out wide and avoid contact until we are engaged, then they will come in to support us."

It took another twenty minutes or so for the Ottoman ships to close in. Marty had to admit it was a well-executed manoeuvre by the three corvettes.

"French built," Gordon McGivern said.

"Probably sold off after the war was over," Wolfgang said.

"What do you think they will do?" the general asked. He was impressed with the calm, cool nature of the officers.

"Probably order us to heave to so they can board and search us."

"What are they looking for?"

"Why, I thought that was obvious. They are looking for you." Marty didn't try and tell him to go below, instead watched as the Port Corvette swung around to come abeam of them. The other two stayed to windward.

An officer shouted something in Turkish using a speaking trumpet. Georges translated. "He says that we have to stop and be searched."

"Tell him we will not, and we will defend ourselves," Marty said.

The corvette's gun ports opened, and her guns ran out. Marty nodded to Wolfgang.

"Run out the port guns."

Marty watched the officers on the corvette's quarterdeck as the big eighteen pounders emerged. He chuckled, "I think that caught them by surprise."

Something pricked him in the back. He lowered the telescope slowly. A hand held his collar, stopping him from moving away.

"Tell them to pull the guns in and stop the ship," a gruff voice said.

The quarterdeck was a frozen tableau. The general and Georges were staring at Marty open mouthed in surprise. Wolfgang had his hand on a pistol butt, a hard look on his face. The helmsmen stood at the wheel unaware of what was happening. The midshipman, busy watching the schooners.

Marty turned his head slowly and saw that it was the general's batman.

"You speak English?"

"I do, give the order, or I will kill you."

"Nico, the kanis?" the general asked in Greek.

"Skasse anoite," Nico snarled.

"You work for the Ottomans?"

"Yes, now give the order."

"I'm afraid I cannot do that," Marty said.

"Then he can. Captain, give the order to stop and run in your guns or I will kill your commodore."

"Go ahead, it won't make any difference. I will kill you and we will deliver the general," Wolfgang said.

Marty spotted a movement above them in the rigging but didn't react. The knife in his back was digging in uncomfortably and he could feel a trickle of blood running down. A shadow passed over him. There was a howl of pain from behind him followed by a thud. The knife was no longer a problem.

Marty turned around. Chin, butterfly swords in hand, stood over Nico who knelt on the deck holding the stump where his hand had been. The hand, still holding the knife, lay on the deck.

"Thank you, Chin," Marty said calmly then said to a ship's boy, "please ask Mr Shelby to come to the quarterdeck." He took a length of cord and applied a tourniquet to Nico's arm. "We don't want you bleeding out now do we."

He turned his attention back to the corvette. There was a lot of arm waving on the quarterdeck, then a shouted order. Their guns elevated.

"They're going for our rigging."

Wolfgang shouted an order, and the carronades were uncovered just as the corvette fired, causing minor damage to the Unicorn's rigging. The Unicorn replied with a full broadside aimed at their hull.

The carronades chuffed on the foredeck and the bow of the corvette disintegrated as two sixty-four-pound balls hammered into it, the quarterdeck thirty-two-pound carronades fired and swept the corvette's quarterdeck clean with canister.

On the windward side the other two corvettes were moving in. One to bracket the Unicorn the other towards the Neaera. Further out the Eagle and Endellion reacted by closing in, guns at the ready.

"Run out the starboard guns, Mr McGovern," Wolfgang ordered.

The port guns roared again. At almost point-blank range the corvette didn't stand a chance. Her main mast broke below the main deck and, as it toppled, ripped a huge hole in the deck planking. The stays connecting the main to the fore and mizzen masts shivered under the strain. Something had to give. The mizzen, being the smallest and most slender, snapped halfway up and the main went over the side.

The second corvette was coming in fast. As soon as it could turn to bring its guns to bear, nine-pound balls slammed into the Unicorn's hull but at that range did little damage.

"Port battery, fire as you bear!" Wolfgang shouted.

Shelby came on deck and immediately ordered Nico to be taken below. Chin and Antton picked him up and took him down for Annabelle to attend to. He turned his attention to Marty who had a spreading red patch on his back near his kidneys.

"Take off your shirt."

"In the middle of a battle?" Marty grinned.

Shelby just looked at him.

"Alright, alright. Don't nag."

Nico's knife had cut an inch long hole that was a half to three quarters of an inch deep.

"You will have another scar. I need to stitch it."

"It can't wait?"

"No."

Shelby swabbed it with a clean piece of muslin soaked in raw alcohol. Marty didn't move. The general moved around to see what was happening. Shelby was threading a medium-sized curved needle with silk. Once ready, he started stitching the wound. Again, Marty didn't move or flinch. Four stitches that reached down into the wound pulling it closed all the way down into the muscle were sufficient. A dressing and bandage were applied, and a clean shirt put on, Marty was ready to continue with the fight.

Hector appeared and sat by Marty's left foot. Adam came up from the cabin looking for him.

"Leave him, he is not bothered by the guns," Marty said.

Adam disappeared then reappeared with his and Marty's rifles.

Marty took his and the two started shooting at the marksmen in the corvette's tops some hundred and fifty yards away. It was more to suppress them than in any hope of killing one. Both ships were moving so a hit would be pure luck.

The guns roared again and were echoed by the Neaera's guns aft of them. Then the schooners arrived and positioned to cut off any escape for the corvettes.

"What do you want us to do? We can capture them or sink them," Marty said to the general.

"Capture them, our navy can use them if you take them to Crete." The general was genuinely impressed at the fighting ability of the ships and the way they worked together.

The first corvette was beyond saving and sinking by the bow. They ignored it and closed with the second.

"Prepare to board. Carronades sweep the deck."

The gun crews loaded with canister turning the carronades into massive anti-personnel weapons. They turned the guns on their pivots, aiming to fire along the deck as they came alongside. They fired when the ships were just twenty feet apart. The effect was grizzly and devastating.

"Boarders away!"

Marty swapped his rifle for pistols and followed Wolfgang over the side. Hector was tied to the mizzen and barked furiously, struggling to get free as Marty judged he was too young to get into a real fight.

Marty and Wolfgang were side by side, facing men who came up from below decks. Marty shot one in the chest with his left pistol and blew the brains out of another with his right. A third man rushed him thinking he had empty guns. He was stopped dead by a pair of bullets from the second barrels of the Mantons that turned his lungs to pulp.

The Eagle had come up on the corvette's other side and boarded. Outnumbered, the Ottoman crew threw down their weapons. They were rounding them up and disarming them when Hector appeared beside him, the remnants of the line that had tied him hanging from his collar. Marty inspected it thinking he had snapped it but it was wet having been chewed through.

Behind them the third corvette was still being contested by the Neaera and Endellion. The Neaera's marines were attacking in waves. The corvette's crew realised they didn't stand a chance and struck.

"What do you want to do with the prisoners?" Marty asked the general who had drawn his scimitar and joined in.

"Please take them to Crete with you. They can be held there."

Marty took him back aboard the Unicorn. Hector followed, leaping the gap with ease. Marty sent a boy down to the surgeon to enquire about Nico.

Down in his cabin he gently questioned the general.

"Did Nico give you any reason to suspect him?"

"No, he has been with me for the last three years. I am astonished that he is an Ottoman agent."

"I think we can assume he was the one who told the Ottomans we were taking you back by ship. He needs to be interrogated. Will you leave that to me?"

"I will, but I want him back alive so we can make an example of him."

"We won't kill him."

There was a knock at the door and Shelby stepped in.

"Your assassin is stable. He lost some blood when Chin amputated his hand but thanks to your tourniquet not as much as he could have."

"Is he in shock?"

"Slightly. He needs to be watched for the next day. Why? Do you want to interrogate him?"

"If we can, we need to find out what he has told the Ottomans."

"Can it wait a day?"

"By then we will be anchored and the general and the marines will be on their way to the encampment. They will take him with them for trial and execution." Shelby nodded and went to release his patient.

The prisoner was brought into the cabin with a hood over his head. The general watched from a corner. Marty walked around him. Then lent in close and whispered in his ear.

"What is your name?"

There was no answer.

"I will ask one more time. What is your name?"

There was still no answer.

Marty nodded to Antton and Matai who stepped up and started pushing him and shouting questions.

"What is your name?"

"Where were you born?"

"Are you married?"

He stoically absorbed the abuse.

"It's time we upped the pressure," Marty said after ten minutes of this.

Nico was forced down onto the floor and held there by the Basques. Marty took a jug of water and poured it steadily over Nico's face concentrating on his mouth and nose. The hood stuck to his face as he gasped for breath. Matai punched him in the stomach, driving any air out of his lungs. He threw up into the hood.

Marty kept pouring until the jug was empty. They dragged him to his feet. Matai and Antton pushing and shoving him and shouting questions.

"What is your name?"

"Are you married?"

"What is your father's name?"

Marty stepped in.

"That's enough, boys."

Nico stood swaying. The treatment was repeated when he still refused to answer. After an hour of this, Marty said, "Now we will start again. We have all day and can keep this up indefinitely. What is your name? You aren't giving anything away by telling us that."

"Nicolai, Nicolai Kalchik."

"That does not sound Greek."

"Serbian, I am a Serbian."

The general looked surprised.

"When did you start working with the general?"

"Three years ago."

"Were you an agent then?"

"Yes, can I sit down?"

"When you answer all my questions."

"How did you get into the Greek army?"

"I just walked in and joined."

"When was that?"

"Four years ago."

"Why do you work for the Ottomans?"

"My mother is a Turk."

"What is her name?"

"Gulya."

"That's a pretty name, what does it mean?"

"It means flower."

"Who is your contact in Ottoman Intelligence?"

Nico was swaying. The smell of his vomit leaked from the hood. Inside it must have been unbearable.

"I need to rest."

"I know. You can rest after you tell me who your contact is."

He swayed and the boys roughly forced him to stand upright.

"Jerzy."

"Jerzy who?"

"Jerzy Bouras."

There was a gasp from the corner.

"Clean him up then take him back to the surgeon," Marty said and when he was gone turned to the general. "You know that name?"

"I do, he is the mayor of Gravia."

"Looks like he is on the Ottoman's side. If I were you, I would set a watch on Mayor Bouras and find out who else is feeding him information. You can take him out whenever you want after that."

"Can you do it? He knows all my men."

Marty considered that, weighing the advantages against the disadvantages.

"I can leave two of my men here until I return from the islands. They are experts in surveillance. You will also be getting a retired marine captain, Paul La Pierre, as an advisor. He has fought many battles and is one of the most experienced men I know."

Chapter 12: Crete

They left the Gulf of Malian and headed out into the Aegean with the northerly wind in their favour as they could sail with it on their stern. Their next stop would be Crete and the southern port town of Kokkinos Pirgos where they had been told they could hand over the prizes. The Ottomans had a strong presence in Heraklion and the main ports along the north coast which they had garrisoned.

They sailed into port to see a number of warships tied up flying the Greek flag. Georges told them, "This is the home of the Greek Navy. The Ottomans don't get near here and have no idea that we have it."

Marty doubted that. The Ottomans clearly had an efficient spy network and probably knew as much as Georges did. They anchored and Georges went ashore to talk to the commander of the small fleet. He returned with him in tow.

"Lord Martin, may I introduce Admiral Costas Philippoussis, Commander of the Navy."

"Pleased to meet you. Please call me Costas," the commander said.

"Then please call me Martin. Your English is very good."

"I was a lieutenant in the Royal Navy until 1816 when my ship was laid up. I know of you and your record in the war, Martin."

"I am just a private individual at this time."

"Yet you still appeared on the navy list as late as last year." Costas grinned. "Don't worry, we will uphold the fiction. Now you have some ships for me?"

"Yes, those two corvettes. There were three but one succumbed to our guns."

"You have repaired them, I see."

"There are repairs that still need to be done but they sail well enough. There are prisoners that need to be taken over."

"We will take care of them. I will send crews aboard and you can have your men back."

The corvettes taken care of, Marty asked Georges to contact the rebels so they could send marines ashore. He returned with three bishops: Constantine, Dimitris, and Nicholas. "It is the Christian population that will revolt. The Ottomans have converted many to Islam some of which are faithful to their new creed, others only converted because of the economic incentives and still secretly worship Christ," Bishop Nicholas, who was their spokesman, explained in English.

Crypto-Christians, Muslim on the outside, Christian on the inside, Marty thought.

"The northern cities are predominantly Muslim. The revolt will come from the mountains and the south."

That made sense as the peasants were much less likely to convert than merchants who had a financial incentive. They would have to use a different method of training as this would be much more of a guerrilla war. Marty explained he had men who were experts in the type of warfare that the rebels on the island would be engaged in and a sergeant who could provide tactical advice.

"With a strong, entrenched enemy you need to fight a guerrilla war to start with to weaken them without sacrificing your own people. Attack their commerce, supplies to the towns they control, stir up unrest amongst the population. Then when you have enough trained men, a simultaneous attack on their strongholds from inside and outside will be effective."

Bishop Nicholas translated for the others who nodded in agreement then had a brief discussion.

"Could we meet the man who will be our advisor?"

Marty sent word for Sergeant Bright to join them. He walked in dressed in uniform with all his ceremonial gold braid on display. The only thing missing were his regimental insignia.

"This is Sergeant Major Bright who will be your advisor. He has fought many guerrilla actions against the French and Spanish."

Bright bowed.

"Are you a spiritual man?" the bishop asked him.

"Aye, Your Grace. I belong to the Anglican High Church."

"A rare breed indeed. Do they still worship in the orthodox manner?"

"We do."

"Then you will be welcome to attend services here. It must have been some time since you have been able to?"

"The life of a sailing soldier has its limitations, Your Grace. I attend when I can."

This was all news to Marty as in all the years he had known Bright they had never discussed religion.

Marty decided to stay in Crete for a while and asked Georges to take him, Bright and Antton to Heraklion so they could get a first-hand look at the defences. It was evident that there wasn't a senior military commander amongst the rebels who had any combat experience at all.

They wore brown vraka, baggy trousers, tucked into knee-length boots, a white poukamiso, loose shirt made of cotton and a long coat made of wool. On his head Marty wore a koukos skull cap decorated with tassels. Antton wore a fez and Bright went bare-headed. Antton and Marty had been cultivating moustaches since visiting the Ionian Islands and had respectable growth on their top lips. Bright already sported a fine handlebar moustache. They wore their hair loosely tied back Cretan style

Georges got him a horse. A skittish locally-bred Messara gelding who he suspected was a rig (castrated late so kept some of the characteristics of a stallion) and took some firm handling. It was small by British standards, not much bigger than a New Forest pony at thirteen hands but had immense stamina and was sure footed. Antton and Bright looked funny on their ponies, their long legs hanging almost to the floor.

The route to Heraklion took them over the central mountains. A climb of three thousand feet. They left just after dawn and headed west before turning more to the north. They had a local guide supplied by Bishop Nicholas, who was a quiet mountain man who rode a hinny (a cross between a male horse and female donkey).

As soon as they turned north, the land rose steadily until around midday. They came to a village on the small plateau with a taverna in the central square where their guide stopped for lunch. They were served Stifado, a rich stew with lamb, pork and snails, with crusty bread straight out of the oven. Washed down with glasses of fresh spring water and a fortifying glass of Tsikoudia, a tasty grape-based spirit.

While they ate Marty noticed that practically every man carried a musket. It was so common a sight as to seem part of the local dress. He also registered that all the women carried long knives in the sashes they wore around their waists.

Lunch over, they moved on. The locals watched them leave and Marty had the feeling they would be watched all the way out of the mountains. Every so often a piercing whistle would be heard, and their guide would look up into the peaks that surrounded them. Marty moved his horse up beside Georges.

"Are those whistles a signal?"

"Sort of, they are to let the next person along know you are moving into their territory."

"Sentries?"

"No shepherds. The boys that look after the goats and sheep."

As they moved down into a valley the sound of pipes drifted across the air along with the scent of herbs. Marty identified thyme, mint, rosemary and marjoram. He started to look for them and spotted herbs growing everywhere. The sheep grazed on them which explained the wonderful taste of the mountain lamb.

Heraklion was a fortified city built by the Venetians, with a high wall, bastions and redoubts. Cannon poked their noses out through embrasures and men patrolled along the parapets. They circled to the west to get to the main gate which was protected by a fort outside of the high main wall and guarded by a troop of brightly-dressed and turbaned Ottoman soldiers. Marty, Antton and Bright studied them surreptitiously, noting the long-barrelled, bell-mouthed muskets that were heavily decorated with brass inlay on the stocks and butts. The men all carried scimitars either pushed through their sashes or slung from them, and some had axes or long curved knives pushed through the back. Only one carried a pistol and they assumed he must be the officer.

They passed through the gate after receiving only a cursory inspection and entered a wide boulevard. Georges pointed out interesting buildings before turning towards the port. They dismounted at a taverna which had rooms and stables. The owner was a Crypto-Christian and a member of the Filiki.

"We have rooms upstairs looking into the courtyard," Georges said. They took their saddlebags up to their rooms and returned to the common room for dinner. They drank sparingly and checked the room for anyone who might be watching them. They spoke quietly and listened a lot.

"There are people from all over the Mediterranean here," Marty said. "I've heard English, Italian, Spanish as well as Maltese and Arabic."

Two tables over from them were a group of Greek sailors who were drinking heavily. Two tables from them was a group of Egyptians who were drinking tea. The Raki started to speak, and insults and taunts started to fly. The taverna owner looked worried. The taunts were reaching a crescendo when Marty said, "Let's take a walk, it will help our digestion."

As they got to the door there was the crash of a table overturning. By the time they got to the other side of the square soldiers were converging on the taverna as a general melee had broken out.

There was a light breeze that carried the smell of cooking out to sea, but it did little to cover the smell of a mass of humankind concentrated in a city environment.

"Didn't the Venetians know anything about sewers?" Bright said as they negotiated an open trough beside the road with effluent running in it running down to the port.

"In Venice all the shit goes into the canals," Marty said.

"Washes out to sea?"

"Nope, Venice is on a lagoon. What goes out sticks around."

"Stinks then," Bright laughed.

They walked towards the port and passed through a plaza that had a large building next to it.

"This is the Plaza of Arsenals."

"Is that building an arsenal?" Marty said.

"It is, there are two more. One next to this one and one the other side of the port. They are all this big."

A squad of soldiers marched along the path next to the building.

"Heavily guarded," Antton noted dryly.

The port itself wasn't, but there was a castle on an island that could effectively close the port from the sea.

"That beast would be impassable if they closed the port," Marty said.

"It would take a squadron of liners to reduce it," Antton replied.

They walked around the seawall looking for all the world like farmers marvelling at the sight of all the ships. Their conversation was anything but land like.

"Two thirty-six-gun frigates, four xebecs, a corvette, a seventy-four and what is that?" Marty said as a strange-looking ship came into view. What they saw was a three-masted ship, schooner rigged, roughly one hundred and twenty-five feet long and thirty feet wide. Low decked (no fore or stern castles) with eleven main gunports to a side on the gun deck and two eighteens as fore chasers. They couldn't see if it had stern chasers.

"There's a battery of swivels on the main deck. Must be two dozen of them. Three or four pounders," Bright said.

Marty took a small telescope from his pocket and using Antton to shield it from view, scanned the ship quickly.

"It's a highbred galley. There are rowing benches on the main deck. Probably eighteen to twenty pairs."

He folded the telescope and put it back into his pocket.

"She's pretty but what's the point?" Marty said.

They decided to go to a dockside taverna and see what they could find out. They took a table and Georges talked to the barman. They were served wine and olives. Georges told them she was the Pasha's private ship,

"According to the barman he bought it from the Swedes."

"That explains it. It's a bloody Turuma. I've never seen one, only heard about them. They were used in the Baltic in the Swedish Russian conflict," Marty said.

The sun hit the horizon, so they headed back to their taverna after drinking a couple of glasses of wine. They had noticed that nobody but soldiers were permitted to walk the walls and there were guards at the bottom of the steps preventing anyone from trying.

Peace had returned to the taverna. The Greek sailors were gone, and the Egyptians had moved to a table on the edge of the forecourt. A pair of soldiers were conspicuously sitting on the base of a statue in the plaza.

They went to their rooms but Marty and Antton, who shared a room, didn't go to bed. They changed into black one-piece over-suits with hoods that could be pulled down over their faces, soft-soled shoes, and gloves. At two in the morning, they exited via the window and climbed up on to the roof.

Moving from roof to roof they made their way towards the walls. Marty wanted to have a look at the guns. They dropped to ground level when the gap to the next house was too large to jump. Moving quietly and carefully, they made their way to a section of wall where a warehouse had been built close to it.

They slipped into a side door and Marty opened a small, shuttered lamp to light their way. They found stairs to an upper floor and from there up into the loft. There was a hatch that let them up onto the flat roof and he shuttered the lamp before opening it.

Pausing to let his eyes adjust to the dark he listened with the hatch cracked open. Hearing nothing, he gently pushed it. The hinges resisted. Antton dripped oil on them from a small bottle using a hollow straw. Marty gently worked them to get the oil to penetrate then silently opened the hatch and climbed out. Antton followed and they moved to where the roof and the wall were only a few feet apart.

Antton looked up at the parapet that was six feet above them. The silhouette of a guard passed and when he was gone Antton moved. He walked back across the roof, turned, and sprinted towards the edge. At the last moment he jumped and used his momentum to scale the wall and gain a hold on the parapet. A swift pull and he was on it. Marty followed. Antton grabbed his hand and pulled him up.

They went straight to one of the guns and checked it over. It was a twenty-four-pounder mounted on a naval carriage. Well maintained with balls stacked beside it. They took careful note of how far it could be depressed. He paced off to where the next was.

Having seen enough they retrieved their horses and left. As soon as they were safely out of the city Marty briefed Bright and Georges.

"You won't be able to take that city by assaulting it from the outside but if you feign an attack from the south and there was to be an uprising inside that could take the walls it may be possible to open the gates and let in a big enough force to take the city. The castle on the island is impregnable to all intents and purposes. All you will be able to do is bottle them up."

"What about the warships?" Bright asked.

"We will try and lure them out by blockading the port."

Chapter 13: The Network

Veronica sat in the office, as she called it, in the hidden room on the third floor of her house in Zakynthos. On the wall were maps of mainland Greece and Crete covered in little blue, green, yellow and red flags. Billy came in with a sheet of paper in his hand.

"This just arrived," he said and passed it to her.

The thin, tatty sheet had been folded into as small a packet as possible to enable it to be concealed by the courier who was a fisherman from the mainland. It was written in Greek and encoded.

Veronica decoded and translated the message, picked up a red flag and stuck it into the town of Patras.

"Red is a controller?" Billy said.

"Yes, Kostas has followed the trail from the informers we identified in Drosato and Kato Achaia to Patras and identified an Ottoman merchant."

"There isn't much going on over there is there?" Billy said looking at the map.

"No, but we can make them think there is when the Greeks are ready to go. We should start thinking about what we want to do there."

"I think we need to make a report to Lord Martin. We have enough details now to give him an idea of the extent of their network. I will get the boat ready, so we can leave as soon as you have it prepared."

"How will you find him?" veronica asked.

"They will have a ship waiting at a particular place on the fifteenth of the month. All I have to do is be there at the same time."

"It's the twelfth, today. Do you have enough time?"

"If I leave tomorrow early."

Veronica sighed; it looked like she would have to work all night.

Veronica started by taking duplicate maps and replicating all the pins in coloured inks. Beside each was a series of letters which represented basic information on each contact followed by a number. The number referenced her notes on the contact which she copied into a small book. If that wasn't enough work, she had to encrypt the notes by lantern light.

Dawn came and Billy went into the office to see how she was doing. He found her, head on arms fast asleep. He checked the notebook and it stopped in the middle of a sentence. She hadn't finished it.

Veronica woke up with a start.

"It's alright, it's me," Billy said.

"Oh, I must have fallen asleep." She looked at the notes. "I haven't finished them."

"How much is left to do?" Billy said.

"About a quarter."

"Come on, you can finish it on the boat."

Veronica collected the notes that she had left to encode, locked the ones that had been completed in the safe, grabbed a box of pens and a bottle of ink and followed Billy out. He grabbed some clothes from her closet and stuffed them in a bag along with her "essentials".

The boat was large enough to need five men to sail her. Marty had provided a master's mate and five hands. Billy was only rated as a landsman, so Stan Guildford was the skipper, with Bill Crow, Taff Jones, Titch Bowden, Nipper Crow and Nathaniel Baldwin as crew. Billy helped but was effectively a passenger.

Veronica climbed aboard and looked around. There was a small cabin aft of the mast. The rest of the boat was open. It suddenly occurred to her that she would be spending at least the next two days on it.

"Billy," she said tentatively.

"Yes, love?" he said as he helped pull the sail up.

"Where is the toilet?"

"Hmm?" he said as the sail reached the top of the mast and the boat moved out into the bay.

"Where is the toilet?"

He turned, and as he did, he saw the grins on the lad's faces.

"Oh, I never thought about that."

She placed her hands on her hips and glared at him.

"Am I to go over the side like the rest of you?"

"Aah, ummm," Billy stuttered, going red.

Stan stepped up and rescued him.

"We can put a bucket in the cabin for you, miss, and Billy can rig a piece of sailcloth over the door, so you have some privacy like."

"Thank you, Stan." She smiled, then gave Billy a withering look.

"Only to be used when it's calm, mind." Stan's ability to keep a straight face was tested.

Veronica suspected she was being teased but Stan was a picture of innocence and Billy was still blushing. She looked in the cabin which had a single bunk and a table. There was a bench down one side.

"I will be working in here." She turned to go inside and banged her head on the top of the door frame. She huffed, ducked inside and set up her things. The men all found something to do away from the doorway.

The rendezvous was off the northern point of the island of Kithira and they had about a day and a half to get there. Stan had calculated that as long as the wind held steady, they would be there in twenty to thirty hours. However, the sea is a fickle mistress, and the wind dropped that evening reducing their speed to a crawl. On the upside it was calm allowing Veronica to finish her work.

Come the dawn the wind increased, and they set every piece of canvas they could. Running the log showed they were making nine knots. The absolute maximum for the boat. They came into sight of Kithra at a quarter before noon and they were spotted by the lookout on the Endellion at ten minutes past.

Veronica couldn't care less. She had gotten seasick when they turned east, and the boat started to corkscrew as it ran at an angle across the swell. She had long ago thrown up all the contents of her stomach and was now dry retching over the leeward gunnel. She was still there when the boat pulled up beside the Endellion.

"Can we get her aboard, Sir?" Billy asked Phillip Trenchard, Master and Commander, "She is really sick."

"Absolutely, old boy. The commodore wants to see her anyway."

Before she knew it Billy was lifting her into a bosun's chair, and she was dangling over the boat. She gently landed on the deck, the sailors being extra careful with Billy in attendance. Billy held out his hand to help her stand. The steady deck of the Endellion, steady compared to the boat that is, had an almost miraculous effect on her and her stomach settled.

"Miss Southerland, pleased to meet you," Trenchard said and bowed. "Could I tempt you with a cup of tea?"

She gulped back a surge of bile.

Below in his cabin, a cup of sweet tea in hand, Veronica listened as he brought her up to date.

"So, you see, we are training their men and have intercepted an informer or two. The Shadows have been busy tracking any known informants to map out the network near the armies. The boss thinks that if we add that information to yours, we will have a pretty good idea of their overall network."

"What do you want us to do?" Billy said.

"You come with us, send the, what is it called?"

"Karavi, it is Greek for boat."

"How droll. Send the boat back to the island with instructions to meet us here in two weeks on the twenty-ninth."

Sailing in the Endellion was infinitely better than the Karavi. It rolled gently compared to the bouncing motion of the boat and she had her own cabin. Actually, it was Trenchard's sleeping quarters, but she had privacy and could use his private head. She went over her notes, clarifying some points and rewriting others.

She had a sponge bath and changed into sailor's slops which Billy sourced for her while her dress was washed by Trenchard's steward. She didn't know it, but she looked a picture in the loose trousers that hugged her hips and a shirt that had been loaned by one of the sailors. It was his best and had laces at the top half of the front and had been embroidered with fantastic marine animals. It followed her curves and the laces showed just a tantalising glimpse of her cleavage.

Trenchard's eyes widened for a second before he got control as she came on deck. Billy, who was chatting to some of the crew, was forewarned by a "Phwor! Would you look at that!" He had to admit she looked good, especially to a woman-starved sailor. Her hair shone in the sun and the shirt was just translucent enough to show her silhouette.

Work had stopped on the deck as every eye turned on her. Veronica blushed and Billy came up to the quarterdeck with a "Permission to come up, Sir?' Trenchard just nodded. Billy took off his jacket and put it around Veronica's shoulders as he whispered in her ear. Her blush deepened.

"Thank you, Billy," Trenchard said, then bellowed, "back to work you lubbers!"

"I'm sorry, Captain, I didn't mean to disrupt the workings of your ship," she said.

"Think nothing of it, Miss Southerland." *The whores at the next port we stop at will have a rare old time of it*, he thought. However, the sailors would have to work off their frustrations as they wouldn't be getting shore leave for a while yet.

They sailed into Kokkinos Pirgos and anchored close to the Unicorn. Billy saw from the set of her yards that she was ready for sea and when they boated across the deck was all a bustle as the men made final preparations to sail. They were taken straight down to Marty's cabin.

"Veronica, welcome! I was hoping you would report in person." Marty rose to greet her.

"I have a full report, Milord," she said a little nervously. Marty still intimidated her, somewhat.

"Excellent, we will get into that once we have sailed."

They heard the first lieutenant bellowing orders. Marty grinned and said, "Come on, we can watch the departure." He led them up to the main deck. Men were up on the yards loosening the harbour gaskets. The capstan clinked as twenty-five men heaved on the bars to the tune played by a fiddler.

"Anchor up and down!"

"Set jibs and fore topsails, set the spanker."

"Anchor away!"

"Catch her, helm!"

"Steerage!"

"Set the mains and royals."

The frigate heeled as she caught the wind, and a fine moustache of white water decorated her bow. Her attendant schooners and the Neaera were in close attendance like bridesmaids to a bride. Veronica realised she had been holding her breath. It was as beautiful as an opera and as coordinated as a ballet.

"Quite a sight, isn't it?" Marty said.

"It is beautiful," Veronica replied. "I can see why you men get so attached to your ships."

"We will head back up to Kamena and get Matai and Garai's report on what they have found. Now let's see what you have discovered."

Back in the cabin Marty spread out the map that Veronica had prepared. He examined it with the aid of a magnifying glass.

"Long vision is as good as ever but I need a bit of help close up," he smiled, "I'm not getting any younger."

He spent two hours going over the map and notes. Veronica was impressed that he could read the encrypted notes without having to write them down.

"Think of encryption as just another language like Greek. Once you have learnt it, reading it becomes easy."

That gave her food for thought as she had made no attempt to learn the code in that way.

"This gives me several ideas which I need to think over then discuss with the generals."

The trip north to Kamena was not easy. They had to sail east for two hundred and eighty miles before turning north of northwest to make the Straits of Artemiseou. In all, it took three days before they anchored where they had before. Matai and Garai were waiting for them at the general's headquarters.

Veronica, dressed in traditional Greek costume, caused somewhat of a stir as she entered the camp. There were women there that had followed their men and others who had set up professionally but none who looked like her. The general gave her a particularly lecherous smile but was perfectly courteous afterwards.

"The mayor is the local controller and collector of information. We identified three more informants who were visiting him regularly. He sends reports via a monthly messenger ship that runs back and forth to Constantinople."

"Where they end up on the desk of the Ottoman head of intelligence," Veronica added.

"Do we know who that is?" Marty said.

"No one does. His identity is a closely-guarded secret."

Marty turned to the general.

"Who knows that you intend to start the uprising in June?"

"Only the leadership of the Filiki Eteria."

"But Nico must have heard you talking to them about it. He was with you all the time."

"My god! Yes, he would," the general gasped.

"Then we can assume that the Ottomans know it as well."

Chapter 14: Corfu

Captain James Campbell returned to his ship and barked orders. They would sail from Gibraltar immediately. His meeting with Admiral Moore had been brief. The admiral had made it obvious that he didn't like the idea that the Leonidas and Nymphe would be acting independently but accepted that the First Sea Lord had his reasons.

James, and his fellow captain Andrew Stamp of the Nymphe, were well aware that the fierce loyalty of the men to their captains and ultimately their commodore was one reason that some senior officers of the navy wanted the flotilla disbanded. In particular Admiral Gambier, who was very well connected politically, had a personal dislike of the commodore because of his friendship with Thomas Cochrane and their action at the Battle of the Basque Roads.

Now they would move to the port of Corfu which would be their base for the rest of their deployment. From there they would patrol the coast of Greece and the Aegean Sea. Publicly they would be part of the Ionian squadron but in reality, they were independent and at the call of Commodore Stockley.

Fully provisioned with ample fresh, full mangers and fresh water in new iron tanks this should be a comfortable cruise. The preparatory signal for making sail was raised and acknowledged by their consort.

"Execute," James barked.

The Frigate and Sloop of War, heeled as the wind caught their sails and in perfect synchronisation arced out of the harbour under full sail. Knowledgeable onlookers admired the sight of the elegant ships racing out of harbour like greyhounds after a hare and appreciated the skill required. Vice Admiral Graham Moore watched from the quarterdeck of the Caledionia. He also admired the seamanship and symmetry of their exit while muttering, "Flashy frigate captains" for the benefit of his flag captain.

The cruise to Corfu was uneventful. To keep the men honed they exercised the guns and practised sail and mast evolutions every day. James ran a taught ship, firmly but with a brand of leadership that meant every man would do their utmost for him and their ship and follow him to hell and back if that's what he asked. Andrew Stamp also had that quality which was not surprising as they had both been trained by the same man.

The fortress on the headland/island as they entered Corfu was massive. Built by the Venetians to withstand the Ottomans. The walls rose directly out of the sea for some fifty feet with two further forts above them. The whole was separated from the mainland by a man-made sea channel. A building shone in the sun and James swung his glass to examine it. It was the church of St George, built in the classic Greek style of white stone with Doric columns across the entrance. From there he shifted his gaze up to the highest of the two forts where stood the lighthouse.

They anchored in the shadow of the fortress on its northern side in Corfu harbour. There were several other ships in port: HMS Benbow, seventy-four-gun third rate was the commodore's flagship, HMS Cambrian, forty-gun fifth rate and three thirty-six-gun fifth rates, Emerald, Naiad, and Shannon.

"Signal from the flagship, our number and captain to repair aboard," Midshipman Essex reported. A second signal flew up the Benbow's halliards, "That was for the Nymphe, same signal."

James had anticipated this and was dressed in his number one uniform with a copy of his orders, a letter from the First Lord of the Admiralty and his commission in his pocket.

"Bring my barge around if you please, Simon."

"Aye, aye, Sir," Simon Fitzwarren, First Lieutenant, replied.

He arrived at the Benbow thirty seconds ahead of Andrew's longboat and had just finished being greeted when Andrew stepped up onto the deck.

"If you will follow me. Commodore Strickland is waiting in his cabin." Captain Reacher led them aft.

Strickland was a man in his fifties who had been a frigate captain. He didn't have much of a combat record as during the war as he had been attached to the Channel Fleet and run messages for the blockade of Brest. James had ten times his experience and he knew it. He made no attempt to greet them apart from a nod and held out his hand for their orders. James and Andrew exchanged a brief glance then stood eyes front while the commodore read them.

"You are to proceed independently?" he said.

"Aye, Sir."

"To what end?"

"To support the Special Operations Flotilla of British Intelligence, Sir."

"And who commands that?"

"Commodore Stockley under the orders of Admiral Turner, Sir."

"That pair of pirates."

"Sir?"

"I know Stockley, I was at the Basque Roads with Admiral Gambier when he and Cochrane went on the rampage."

James said nothing, it was clear that Strickland was either a supporter or a follower of Admiral Gambier.

"Were you there?"

"Yes, I was."

Strickland glared at him. Reacher coughed.

"What is it?" Strickland snapped.

"The letter from the First Lord, Sir."

"What? Oh that." Strickland picked up an envelope and removed the sheets of paper inside and unfolded them. His frown deepened.

"It would appear you are all under orders from the highest level. You are to wait here for Norwich. She will be attached to you and is under my orders."

That was obviously a sap to his pride.

They had a pleasant time in Corfu. The old town was a maze of narrow streets full of stores and taverns. The men soon found where the best drink could be had and discovered locally-made Raki. That led to a number of altercations causing James to cancel leave and lecture the men on their behaviour.

"I will not have the commodore use your behaviour to cause problems for the flotilla. Drink by all means, but in moderation. You know how strong the local spirits are now so there is no excuse for drunken behaviour. Anyone who disgraces himself and thereby his ship will incur my full and unforgiving wrath. Have I made myself clear?"

The men grunted a reply.

"I do not believe I could hear you."

"Aye, aye, Sir."

"Shore patrols will be run by the masters at arms. Carry on."

With the behaviour of his men policed, James took his officers on a sightseeing tour of the ruins of ancient Kerkrya. The ruins were situated on the peninsula that lay due south of Corfu town and originated from several centuries before Christ.

They walked the two-and-a-bit miles to the site and found themselves wandering through ancient walls under fragrant pines and olive trees. They came to what was an amazingly complete theatre and were surprised to see players rehearsing, the acoustics were amazing. Even from the back row they could hear the softest of whispers.

They moved on after listening for a while and found a complete building.

"What do you think it is?" Simon said.

"A temple I should think," Allan Conner, the third lieutenant said.

"Close," a voice said from behind them.

They turned to see a man, wearing a workman's smock over black trousers and sporting a goatee beard. He wore spectacles and carried a board with sheets of paper clipped to it and a box of pencils or charcoals.

"It is in fact a church that was once a basilica. Oh, my name is Peregrine Fortescue-Holmes, Antiquarian, by the way."

"James Campbell, Captain of the Leonidas and my officers, Simon Fitzwarren, Mark James and Allan Conner."

"The Leonidas, eh? Very apt for Greece. Are you interested in the ancients?"

"We all studied ancient Greek, so we have more than a passing interest," James said.

Peregrine was a mine of information and seemed to relish the chance to share it with someone. He explained that the church had once been a tower and part of the city wall. From the thickness of the wall that remained he estimated it must have been some twenty feet high, which meant the tower was probably ten feet higher than that. He also told them that the locals believed that the church was dedicated to Saint Kerkyra, the first woman to be martyred on Crete, and that she protected a fantastic hoard of treasure hidden in the crypt.

"Lord! We should start an excavation." Mark laughed.

"Wouldn't do you any good," Peregrine smiled. "There is absolutely no evidence that a crypt exists, and even if it did the locals would have looted it years ago."

As they parted, he mysteriously said, "Oh and give my regards to Commodore Stockley when you see him." Then he disappeared into the shadows

They walked back to the ship as evening fell and stopped at a restaurant for a meal. They were served fried fish swimming in a sea of fragrant sauce flavoured with olive oil, garlic, vinegar, raisons, laurel and rosemary. That was followed by thinly-sliced pieces of veal that were sauteed and served with a white wine sauce of garlic, parsley and pepper. It was served with leafy greens that were spicy and warming. The dessert was an amazing dish of cubes of thin layered pastry filled with nuts and soaked in syrup.

Full and satisfied they returned to the ship to find it in a state of alert.

"Report, Mr Rathbone," James said to the duty midshipman.

"We had to repel boarders, Sir," Felix said, standing rigidly to attention.

James looked over his shoulder to where some of the crew were looking far too innocent and concealing smirks.

"Oh, and who was attempting to board my ship?"

"Boat loads of women, Sir."

James kept a straight face while the unfortunate midshipman blushed.

"Women? And where did these women come from?"

"From the town, Sir."

"Aah, Syrens or Amazons then."

Simon had a coughing fit and went aft to check for a fictional boat.

"Not exactly, Sir. More like whores."

James looked up at the mast and said, "I do not see a wreath. This ship is not out of discipline."

"Exactly, Sir, that's what I told them, but they insisted on coming aboard."

"So, you called the ship to quarters to keep them off?"

"I did, Sir."

"That is a reasonable thing to do. Have you searched the ship to ensure none remain behind?"

"No, Sir."

"Then please do and have any sailors that they are found with brought to me."

Felix was about to leave when James asked, "When did the last watch return from shore leave?"

"Around a bell before the women came across, Sir."

Fifteen minutes later Felix returned with the master at arms, a pair of women and four sailors. The women were drunk and screaming imprecations in Greek. The men, also drunk, meek at being brought before their captain.

"I am holding you two responsible for this behaviour and the attempted invasion of my ship. You will be flogged in the morning for being drunk and having stowaways on board. The rest of your watch will be denied shore leave for a week and have their rum and tobacco rations quartered. Mr Chester, please throw these harridans over the side then put these men in irons."

James could see the funny side of what happened but the discipline on his ship was more important. He disliked flogging and would decide on the number of lashes when he had a cooler mind. He noticed that any hint of smirks had disappeared.

The next morning, he gathered the crew to witness punishment. The four men were brought forward and lined up in front of the quarterdeck. A grating had already been raised in preparation.

"That you are guilty is beyond doubt. Do any of your shipmates have anything to say in mitigation?"

James scanned his eye along the faces lined up before him. Some were openly hostile towards the condemned and others bland faced or sympathetic. Nobody spoke up.

"Very well, you are sentenced to two dozen lashes each in accordance with articles two, thirty-five and thirty-six of the articles of war."

This was a harsh but not unusual punishment and in this case two burley bosun's mates were tasked to deliver it. The surgeon oversaw it and declared the men fit to receive punishment before strapping a leather apron over their kidneys to protect them.

The mates were chosen, not just for their size, but because one was right-handed and the other left. This was considered more humane as not all the strokes would land in the same direction. The four men received their punishment. Three silently, the last crying out with every stroke.

At the end one stepped forward.

"Captain, Sir. We do humbly apologise for offending your honour and for bringing disgrace to our ship."

James nodded accepting the apology and wondered why they didn't give it before as it might have reduced the sentence.

"The common sailor is a strange fish," Simon said as they discussed it over dinner. "He would rather take his punishment than be seen to grovel to his betters. But at the same time wishes to make it clear that he is sorry for his actions."

"They have their own code of honour belowdecks, we would do well to understand it better," James replied thoughtfully.

James decided that what was needed was to get the ships out of harbour and the men working. So, he sent a message to the commodore that he was taking his ships to sea to exercise them and would return in a month or so. He didn't wait for a reply.

Chapter 15: The Aegean Patrol

The crew settled down quickly once at sea. The punished men returned to duty within a couple of days and James made it clear that the rest of their watch would still have to suffer their punishment when they returned to port.

He sailed his ships hard to the south then around the Gulf of Patras. He decided they would do a survey so had his sailing master check their charts and had a midshipman with a sketch pad in the tops whenever they saw a town. Deep-water soundings were made and compared to the admiralty records. Any corrections would be communicated to the navy cartography office on their return.

The Nymphe slipped into bays, coves and even harbours, her boats sounding the anchorages. She even went and had a look into Patras and listed the Ottoman warships there. They noted the departure of any ships and the flags they sailed under. He left them alone. The time wasn't right to start stirring things up.

From there they slipped into the Gulf of Corinth through the narrows at Patras which were a mere mile and a half wide. An Ottoman warship that looked like it had seen service with the Neapolitan Navy at some time, came out of Patras and settled a mile behind them.

"Anybody would think they don't trust us," James said, making Simon laugh.

They continued their cruise, keeping half an eye on their shadow. Once they had been at sea for almost a month they turned around and started back up the gulf to return to Corfu. Their escort rushed ahead of them.

"Have the lookouts keep a careful watch ahead," James said. They didn't have to wait long before the lookout called, "Sail ahead coming this way. Looks like that frigate that was following us."

"Should I take the ship to quarters?" Simon said.

"Only to preparedness," James said.

The men were already moving to their stations and lounging around as if they were on a make or mend day. James knew better and smiled.

The Ottoman frigate came towards them under full sail then wore in a long arc to come abeam of them. They closed to fifty yards, matching their speed and a man in an ornate turban and rich robes came to the rail.

"English ship," a second less well-dressed man shouted through a trumpet. He pronounced it, 'Engleesh sheep.'

"Could he possibly mean us?" Simon asked.

James looked around. "We are the only sheep here, so he must do." He walked to the rail, picking up a trumpet on the way.

"Can I help you, old chap?" he called.

"What is your name? Who is the captain? And what is your mission?"

James looked around to Simon. "Signal the Nymphe that we will heave to. I'm damned if I am going to communicate by shouting."

The signal given; the Leonidas heaved to, catching the Ottoman by surprise. They had to wear again to get back to them. James watched, assessing their crew's efficiency.

"Would you like to come aboard? We are serving tea," James shouted. The Nymphe, very slovenly, let herself drift.

There was a great deal of bustling on board the Ottoman ship with the richly-dressed man shouting orders.

"Do you think he is the captain?" Simon said, head to one side as he watched the pantomime.

"No, more likely a high-ranking civilian," James said. "Look they have brought a boat around."

The man was hoisted into the boat once it was manned and sat very upright on the second thwart from the back. It was apparent from the way the boat's bow lifted that he weighed quite a bit.

"Rig a chair, double tackle!" Simon shouted.

The boat's oarsmen made a half-decent job of getting him across under the circumstances and the boat pulled up alongside. The chair was lowered, and a pair of sailors made sure their cargo was secure before the landsmen hauled him up and over the side. The second man climbed the battens and timed his arrival to be just after the chair deposited its load gently on the deck.

James and Simon stepped forward and saluted their visitor,

"Captain James Campbell and First Lieutenant Simon Fitzwarren. His Majesty's Ship Leonidas."

The second man translated and said in return, "This is Pasha Ahmad Mahmud Suline. Governor of the Peloponnese. He wishes to know what you are doing here."

"I am very honoured to meet you," James said with absolute sincerity. "Please join me in my cabin for some refreshment."

He led them down to his cabin and bade the Pasha sit. His steward brought in mint tea and sweet biscuits.

"What is your name?" James asked the second man.

"Ozan, Sir." James passed him a glass of tea.

"Now, how can I help his excellency?" Ozan went to reply when James said, as if suddenly remembering their previous exchange, "Oh yes, our mission! Well, you see our admiralty's charts of this region are shamefully out of date and we have come to make sure they are correct. I am a cartographer." He sat back as if that explained everything.

The Pasha scowled and replied, "The gulf is Ottoman. You have no right here."

"Oh, I see. Should we have asked for permission?" James said the picture of innocence. "After all we are only making sure our charts are correct so none of our merchant ships come a cropper."

"Come a cropper? What is, come a cropper?" Ozan asked.

"Have an accident, old boy," Simon drawled. "You know, run aground."

Ozan nodded and translated. The Pasha didn't look convinced for a second.

"You have written orders?"

"Of course," James said and waited.

"Can we see them?"

"Oh! Of course." He went to his desk and made a show of rummaging through a pile of papers. Not finding what he wanted he went to a drawer and with a beaming smile held up an envelope.

"Here you are."

Ozan read them out to the Pasha. "They are very vague."

"Are they? I suppose they are, but that goes with the job. You see they like to give their captains a bit of discretion."

The Pasha ate one of the biscuits watching James all the time as if assessing him. He finished it, took a sip of tea and ate another. He visibly relaxed. He was about to eat a third when he shook himself and stood. The others all jumped to their feet.

"The Pasha says that you must leave the gulf now and if you wish to return have to ask for permission before you enter it. We will return to our ship. He thanks you for your hospitality."

"Please take some of the biscuits for him," James said.

"Well, that went well," Simon said, as they watched the boat return to the Ottoman ship. "I see Andrew is to leeward of them now."

"As he should be and it's not gone unnoticed by their captain."

"Bracketed."

"Indeed."

"The Pasha was much more – mellow – by the time he left."

"Yes, the biscuits were made using an old Dutch recipe."

Simon looked at him with wide eyes.

"Hemp?"

James grinned. "That's why I didn't offer you any."

Simon started to chuckle. He was still chuckling when James went below.

The ships returned to Corfu. The Norwich was in harbour, her crew industriously cleaning her.

"She's not been here long," Simon said.

As soon as they anchored, a boat came across from the Norwich and the reply to the hail told them it was her captain.

"Captain Coats, welcome aboard the Leonidas," James said.

"Thank you, Captain Campbell." Coats smiled. "I have a dispatch for you."

If Coats was delivering it himself, it must be important, so James took him down to his cabin. Coats handed the envelope over and James recognised Marty's writing immediately.

"Can I offer you some refreshment?" He slid a knife under the seal.

"Do you have coffee? I have run out and the local stuff is so strong you can dissolve metal in it."

James called his steward and soon a pot of freshly-brewed coffee was served. It smelt wonderful.

"Is this the same bean that the commodore uses?"

"It is. They are from his own plantation."

James read the letter, glancing up at Coats once who had his eyes closed as he savoured the brew.

"Lord Martin says that you will be accompanying us on patrol."

"Yes, the First Lord decided that you needed an extra ship."

"How did Martin take that news?"

Coats noticed the lack of the honorific. "He was surprised."

"Commodore Strickland said you will be under his orders."

"Technically, yes, to maintain the forms, in reality the First Sea Lord has attached me to your squadron."

"Flotilla," James corrected. "On paper we are part of the Mediterranean fleet."

James wondered if the commodore would use the technicality to make life awkward for Marty.

"We will patrol the Aegean and rendezvous with the flotilla in a month off of the island of Skyros to get further orders."

"I assume we will not be patrolling aimlessly."

James chuckled, "You have met Martin, he has a reason for everything he does. We will be counting Ottoman ships. Especially their warships and those of their allies."

"So, we will be spread out to cover as much sea as possible?"

"Exactly; with three ships we can cover around fifty-five miles of sea."

"I assume we will not engage with any?"

"We will not unless fired on first."

Coats nodded.

"Would you join me for dinner tonight? You can bring your first as well."

"I would be delighted. When will we sail?"

"As soon as we have provisioned and topped off our water, how prepared are you?"

"We will be provisioned and watered by the day after tomorrow."

"Then we will leave then."

At dinner Coats asked them, "Were you at the Basque Roads?"

"I was a lieutenant in command of the Alouette. She was a former French corvette and part of the Special Operations Flotilla at the time."

"Is it true Gambier wouldn't attack?"

"He considered an attack to be foolhardy and to put his men at risk," James answered carefully.

"My uncle said he was a coward."

"Who was your uncle?"

"Captain George Seymour of HMS Pallas. He was there."

"I remember him, he fought with bravery and honour."

"Can you tell me what happened?"

James recounted the battle and how they had used fire and bomb ships. At the end he said, "Gambier never ordered his fleet to engage. His signals were deliberately obtuse and confusing."

"How did Lord Martin avoid his revenge while Sir Thomas Cochrane took the full brunt of it?"

"Thomas tried to take on Gambier through a court martial. However, Gambier managed to load it with his political allies. Martin has powerful friends who made sure he was away at the time, otherwise he would have stood by Thomas. They are still friends."

They would set sail as planned but not before the commodore called James to the flagship and tried to rip him off a strip. James stood impassively and let the man's fury wash over him.

"Sir," he said calmly, "I believe I did you the courtesy of informing you that we would go out to exercise the ships and crews and I returned when I said we would. I am fulfilling the standing orders of Commodore Stockley and keeping my ships in fighting trim."

"Fighting trim?" Strickland bellowed, "To fight what or who? We are at peace man!"

"To fight the enemies of the crown as deemed by parliament and the Prime Minister at any time of their choosing."

"And who might that be at this time?" Strickland was going red in the face.

"That, Commodore, is something you would have to discuss with Commodore Stockley, Admiral Turner, The First Sea Lord or George Canning."

"I have written to the First Lord asking to be told what is going on."

"I can tell you no more than I have."

"Then get out!" the man shouted, spraying a shower of spittle.

James saluted and left.

Strickland waited until he heard the side party whistle James off the ship then called for his flag captain.

"Reacher, I want to know what those pirates are up to. Have the Skua follow them with orders to keep them in sight at all times."

"Sir, is that wise?"

"Dammit, man, do as I say."

"Deck there! There's a sail behind us. Comes into sight then ducks back behind the horizon. Looks like a cutter's topsail."

Simon handed over a guinea to James. "You were right, he set someone to follow us."

"It will be the Skua. It's the only cutter he has. Ignore it."

"I will keep an eye on it if you don't mind, Sir. You never know it might get into trouble."

They were sailing up the Aegean from just north of Crete in a series of long tacks as the wind was against them. The Leonidas was in the centre with the Nymphe to port and the Norwich to starboard. The current tack was to the northwest, and they were approaching the coast of the Island of Euboea. James was about to order the ships to tack to the northeast when the Nymph fired a gun.

"Signal the Norwich to close up. Helmsman close with the Nymph they have seen something."

"Nymphe has hove to and signalling," the lookout called down.

"Mr Hudson, take a glass up and see what the signal is."

The youngest mid grabbed a glass and slung it over his shoulder. He shot up the ratlines and around the futtock shrouds with the agility of a monkey.

"Wreckage in the water," he called down.

James understood, there had been only fair weather, so any wreckage had to be the result of an action.

It took almost forty-five-minutes to reach the stationery Nymphe and James brought them to within hailing distance.

"What have you found, Andrew?"

"Looks like an Ottoman corvette came up against something bigger and lost."

"How long ago?"

"Long enough for there to be no bodies."

"Preserve any evidence then let us know when we can resume the patrol." He turned to Simon. "Signal the Norwich to hold position."

Their shadow popped up on the horizon then rapidly retreated.

"How far are we off the coast?" James asked the master, Jebediah Griffon.

"About five miles. Outside of what the Greeks claim as their waters."

"What about the current?"

"Follows the coast south, not that fast as it's mostly wind driven."

"So, whatever happened was up the coast to the north."

"Yes. If you want my opinion, the way it was taken apart makes me think of the Unicorn's big smashers."

James took that for consideration.

"We are done here, no bodies but some material that is definitely Ottoman," Andrew Stamp called across.

"We will resume the patrol. Make sail," James ordered.

They continued northeast, aiming for the northern tip of Lesbos and picked up another follower.

"Signal from Norwich, strange sail in sight to the southeast," Midshipman Hudson reported just before dusk.

"Interesting, signal the recall, we will join up for the night," James said and once they were gathered, he asked the captains to report aboard.

"That sail to the southeast, any idea what or who it is?" James asked Coats.

"It looks like a felucca. They don't mind us knowing they are there either and closed to within a couple of miles. We didn't get a clear sight of their flag but from what we could see, it looked Ottoman."

The conversation over dinner was around the wreckage and their shadows.

"The wreckage is definitely a French-built corvette of the type they sold off at the end of the war," Andrew said.

"Then the question is, who sank it?" James said.

"We picked up a lot of pieces of the bow. It looks like it was smashed to pieces by something big."

"Carronades?" Coats said.

"The Unicorn carries two sixty-eight pounders on her fore deck," Andrew explained.

"Two? I didn't see them when I was on her."

"On pivots on the centreline, and thirty-twos on the aft deck as well as her main battery of eighteens," James said. "They were probably covered."

"There was a rather odd structure on her foredeck. Looked a bit like a shed."

James smiled. "That's typical. I expect the walls drop down so they can bring them to bear in moments."

"A corvette wouldn't stand a chance," Coats said.

"And she is sailing with the Endellion and Eagle which are heavily armed and the Neaera which is full of marines," Andrew said.

"What about our shadows?" Coats asked.

"The one behind us is probably courtesy of the commodore in Corfu. He was royally ticked off that we were independent of his command, and ordered to support us. The other is most likely Ottoman and while not a problem now could be later. We do not want them seeing us rendezvous with the rest of the flotilla."

"What can we do? She can sail closer to the wind than us. We could never capture her, and even if we could, the commodore would use it against us," Coats said.

"We will take care of her, when we are ready," James said quietly.

Chapter 16: Training

Paul la Pierre sat in the shade of an awning attached to the general's tent and watched the rebel army being put through their paces by the marines. There was a stark contrast between the professional soldiers' red uniforms and the diverse traditional dress of the locals.

The group closest to him were being taught how to skirmish. They were moving forward in pairs, covering and moving alternately through a training field scattered with boulders and brush. Their instructor fired a shot over one pair's heads, to remind them to keep them down. At the other end of the field was a range where a large group was practising volley fire, in another part, a division practised marching in line.

The general came out and stood looking proudly at his men.

"They are improving."

"They are at that."

"We will soon be able to take on the Ottomans."

"I would advise against getting into a pitched battle. The Ottoman army is battle hardened and professional."

"You would have us hide behind fortifications?"

"If necessary."

"We Greeks do not hide behind fortifications," the general snapped angrily.

Paul kept his thoughts to himself. He and the general had had this conversation before, and the conclusion was always the same. Greek pride would overcome all.

He sighed. *I hope the others are having better luck with their generals.*

Sergeant Bright was indeed having better luck on Crete. The mountain farmers and herdsmen of central Crete were natural guerrilla fighters. He and his men practised ambushes, running battles, raiding, everything a good guerrilla should be able to do. It wasn't long before they started making life difficult for the Ottomans.

The road through the hills passed through a wooded valley and the Ottomans regularly sent large cavalry patrols along it as a show of strength. Their target was one of these patrols led by a particularly nasty individual who thought it fun to ride down suspected partisans after capturing them. They would be given a head start and promised if they could reach a certain point alive, they could go free. Of course, no one ever did.

The ambush was set up at the narrowest point in the valley where fir trees lined the slopes and the road turned sharply around a blind corner. Twenty men were positioned to either side and ten men manned a barricade across the road. Another ten men would drag a second barricade across the road behind the patrol to prevent their escape.

Bright had one of his men at each of the positions to help coordinate the attack. These men would stand beside the local officer and guide him.

The men got into position and Bright stood beside the Greek lieutenant in charge of the force.

"Remember to give clear orders and stay calm," he said to the nervous young man.

A lookout signalled from a hilltop. They were on their way. Bright wore a brown cloak over his uniform and edged his way to a vantage point so he could see down the road. It was a platoon of thirty cavalry. They carried spears and had musketoons in saddle holsters as well as a Kilij (cavalry sabre) through their sashes.

Dimitrios, the young officer, was now visibly nervous and as soon as he saw the cavalry started to raise his arm.

"Not yet, son," Bright said in the calm way of all Sergeant Majors and put his hand on his forearm.

Dimitrios looked at him wide eyed and saw Bright was calmly watching the horsemen advance. He took a deep breath and let it out slowly.

"That's better, let your head lead, not your gut or your nerves."

The soldiers, oblivious to the danger, rode up to and around the corner. The column stopped.

"Now, give the signal."

Dimitrios raised his arm and brought it down sharply. As he did the woods to either side of the column were shrouded in smoke and flame. A tree fell across the road behind the horsemen, manned by men that fired at the rear ranks.

The cavalry was in chaos as horses reared and men fell. There was a whump and a mortar bomb arced over the trees to explode above them. More whumps followed. Another volley from the sides. The crossfire was taking its toll. Musketoons fired back and a man tried to charge the barricade only to be shot out of the saddle. The officer was still alive and spurred his horse at the rear barricade. He seemed invincible as bullets whined passed him. He spurred his horse viciously to make it jump.

Time seemed to slow as the horse took off and arced gracefully over the tree. Not a single bullet touched him until Bright raised his rifle to his shoulder. He was the only marine who carried one as all the others carried the same gun as their students. He cocked it, took aim, led his target, and squeezed the trigger. The 0.625-inch ball took the officer in the right side of the head, passed through his brain and out the other side taking a fair amount of grey matter with it.

The corpse fell off the side of the horse as it landed, its left foot caught in the stirrup. The sudden shift of weight unbalanced the steed and it fell. When it clambered to its feet it stood shaking in shock. A partisan approached it making comforting sounds and holding out an apple.

The disappearance of an entire platoon of cavalry didn't go unnoticed and the Ottoman authorities investigated. No bodies were found but no one could hide the bloody stains on the road. They concluded that the platoon had to have been massacred and reacted in the age-old fashion. They went to the nearest village and hung every man, woman, and child and killed all the animals they could find. Fifty-three people died there and to make up the numbers seven more were taken from the next village and hanged as well.

In Heraklion the Christians were persecuted even more. Random raids on churches, confiscation of goods and internment upped the terror level. The effect? Even more joined the partisans.

In the Peloponnese, Declan O'Driscol and his men had made excellent progress. There was a large and growing army that was big enough to fight a set piece battle. His biggest problem was the number of separate partisan bands that it was made up of. He decided that he would treat them as separate divisions and used that to introduce competition to the training.

One of their deficiencies was in the area of artillery. That is, they had none except for the mortars that the marines had brought with them and there were only four of those. The Ottomans, on the other hand, had large field pieces that were unwieldy but powerful. Most dated from the end of the previous century and were brass.

What the rebels needed was something more portable. Something like a cavalry six pounder, but he had no idea where to get any of those so he started to think of how he could use the mortars instead. The first thing he did was to show them how to attach a cartridge (bag) of powder to the bombs. The charge was weighed to provide a consistent fire and had a fuse inserted. The mortar men would light the fuse, drop the lot in the mortar tube, charge at the bottom and stand back. The charge would ignite the bomb fuse which was cut to the correct length before firing. The manuals that the Toolshed had provided were translated into Greek.

The Greeks loved the mortars and soon had their blacksmiths making replicas. Their version was more of a pot than a tube and not as accurate, but it increased the numbers. Tactics were worked out using skirmishers out front, infantry in line and mortars behind. Declan, being a student of history, knew that Henry V had seven thousand archers at Agincourt and neutralised the threat of a devastating cavalry charge from the French by fronting them with sharpened stakes. So instead of trying to train the men to march into square he had them erect a line of sharpened stakes to protect them from cavalry supplemented by long spears. The choice of battleground would be crucial.

The rate of fire against the Turkish infantry was critical and he worked on getting that up to three volleys a minute. If it worked against the French, he was sure it would work against the Turks.

Chapter 17: Epidemic

Wolfgang watched the Ottoman seventy-four approach, it was obviously curious about the pair of ships sailing in line astern. He had ordered the majority of the men, on both ships, to go below to maintain the fiction they were merchantmen. There was no sign of aggression from the Ottoman, but he was prepared to react if necessary.

Marty was below swathed in blankets and sweating, after Corfu he had come down with a fever and he felt terrible. Hector had climbed on to his bed and would not move. Adam had tried to get him off only to almost lose a finger or two when Hector snapped at him.

Shelby and Annabelle were in attendance. Annabelle laid a hand on Marty's forehead and checked the pulse in his wrist.

"Pulse is elevated, and he is very hot," she said.

"Influenza without a doubt," Shelby replied.

Adam came in with a pot and bowl on a tray.

"Chicken soup?" Annabelle said.

"Rolland's mother's recipe."

"What's in the pot?"

"Hot water, I thought you would want to infuse some herbs."

Annabelle nodded, took the pot to the table then went to her box of medicines.

"Yarrow, white willow and echinacea, I think."

She measured the dried herbs into the pot and stirred for five minutes to make a tea. She poured some into a cup then covered the pot with a cloth. She presented Marty with a spoonful.

"Open wide."

He glared at her but did as he was told, and she dosed him.

"Again."

"I'm not a child," he sniffed.

She ignored him and popped the teaspoon into his mouth then turned to Adam. "Two teaspoons every hour until his fever breaks. Keep him wrapped and isolated. We don't want this spreading through the ship." It was a forlorn hope as Shelby believed that more crew than Marty had been exposed to the disease which was incredibly contagious. It was a blessing that Veronica and Billy had already left.

Out on the horizon the Eagle and Endellion were holding position with the grace of leashed hounds ready to rush to their aid if needed. On deck Wolfgang watched the seventy-four close to a cable to run down their windward side. He could see the officers examining them through telescopes, so he waved. Behind him the Swedish flag cracked as it whipped in the wind.

The Ottomans had slowed and had a lot of men on deck. Wolfgang watched for any sign they were at, or going to, quarters. Along the Unicorn's gundeck the men sat, out of sight ready to go to quarters at a moment's notice.

The seventy-four passed and they all breathed a sigh of relief. Wolfgang noted the name, Fhati Bhari, and wrote it in the log. However, they weren't out of the woods yet as she was closing on the Neaera. She moved into half a cable off the Neaera's beam.

"They are looking at her boats," Gordon McGivern said.

"Who wouldn't. They are unique."

"You never said if the commodore had come up with a cover story for them."

"For carrying cargo in shallow waters."

Gordon didn't look impressed but said nothing. The Ottoman seemed satisfied and put on more sail. Wolfgang ordered an extra lookout to watch it in case they tried to loop back on them. The men stood down and returned to their normal duties

Shelby and Annabelle came up on deck.

"How is the commodore?" Wolfgang asked.

"He is very ill with influenza, has a fever and is wishing he could die right now. He complains of joint pain, his chest is congested, and he has a really bad headache. Adam will look after him from now on and there is to be no unnecessary contact."

"Is his life in danger?"

"He is strong so should survive this, but influenza can take anybody. Constant care is essential."

Two days later the first of the crew went down with it. After that it spread through the ship like wildfire and at least half of the crew were sick. Wolfgang and Richard Brasier were the only fit officers after a week. The only good news was that Marty's fever had broken and he was on the way to recovery. The deck was covered in men in various stages of the illness. Shelby concentrated on trying to prevent pneumonia setting in. That was the real killer.

Wolfgang had reduced their speed and flew the fever flag. They couldn't land anywhere with the number of sick men onboard. The Neaera had not avoided the contagion which left the Eagle and Endellion as the only fully fit ships. But that changed one morning when the Eagle pulled up to hail them.

"We have sickness on board," Trevor Archer shouted.

"Mr Shelby will attend you," Wolfgang bellowed back.

It was the influenza. The Endellion, whose crew hadn't spent any time ashore in Crete, was the only ship that was a hundred percent operational. Wolfgang could only hope they stayed out of trouble until it was over.

Marty felt well enough to go up on deck after two weeks. If he was honest, he was as weak as a kitten and wobbly on his feet, but he had had enough of being confined. The feel of the sun on his face was wonderful and invigorating. His pleasure was interrupted by the sight of the loblolly boys sewing corpses into their hammocks.

"How many did we lose?" he asked Richard Brasier who was acting first.

"Seventeen. Three youngsters including Midshipman Mitchell. The rest were mostly older men. We lost the cook and the carpenter."

Antton came up on the quarterdeck.

"Are all the boys well?" Marty asked.

"Only Garai got sick, and he is over the worst of it."

Marty was saddened, losing men for a cause in action was one thing but having them die of disease was something entirely different and something he had worked hard to avoid. It was why he had invited Shelby to be their surgeon/physician in the first place. He was pondering this when the lookout hailed.

"Endellion signalling, strange sail."

"Where is the Endellion?" he asked Richard.

"Five miles off our port bow."

As the target could be another twelve miles beyond that he wasn't unduly worried. He was more concerned that they needed to get to the rendezvous off of Skiathos. His crew was mainly over the influenza epidemic but many of the men were suffering from chest complaints as a direct result of it. If he could get to the rendezvous, he would sail back to Zakynthos and rest the men for a month.

On the Leonidas, James was pondering as well. The time for the rendezvous was approaching and he had to find a way of losing their Ottoman shadow. He had already tried a few standard tricks like changing course at night after dousing their lights, but the dogged bastard was still there, hull up on the horizon.

He needed to get sneaky and pulled out a chart of the northern Aegean. After a moment's examination he pulled out another.

"Jebediah," he said to get the master's attention, "this island, Lemnos, has a large bay. Have you ever sailed it?"

"Can't say that I have, Captain. Let me look at the admiralty notes."

Jebediah pulled a book titled *The Aegean* from under the chart table and flicked through it.

"Here we are, Lemnos. Hmm. All it do say is that you can water at Moudros."

"Perfect, set a course for Moudros."

Then he went to see the sailmaker. The master watched them talking. The sailmaker laughed and nodded as the captain gave his instructions. Jebediah knew he was up to something but for the life of him he couldn't say what.

Moudros turned out to be a small village with a big church. They anchored off a golden beach and sent empty barrels ashore. The Ottoman followed them in and anchored across the bay. James called on his ancient Greek and sent a message over inviting the captain to dinner. It was declined.

The purser was instructed to source a couple of bullocks that could be slaughtered and roasted over fire pits on the beach. He sent a party ashore to set things up and put the word out in the village that they would be having a party that night.

Come sunset the beach was alive with people and the smell of roasting beef drifted across the bay. The villagers brought instruments and joined with the musicians from the ships. It was somewhat cacophonous but once they all agreed on a rhythm, gave everyone something to dance to. No one noticed the small boat slip out of the harbour and row silently across the bay.

The next morning, they left as soon as it was light enough to see, and once out of the bay piled on the sails. The Ottoman, caught napping, having assumed they would spend an extra day to get over the night before, had to set all sail and race after them. He had built up a fine head of speed when the ship suddenly slowed abruptly, her mast bending under the strain. Rigging snapped. Then she turned and slowed to a halt.

"Deck there, I think the Ottoman must have run aground," the lookout called.

James looked smug and the master looked at him questioningly.

"Someone must have rigged a sea anchor to his steering gear," James smirked.

"Oh, with thin cord holding it shut, so to only let it stream when their ship got up to speed?"

"Something like that."

"The commodore pulled that in the Caribbean."

"Yes, I know."

The rendezvous went to plan. James and Andrew stepped aboard the Unicorn to be reunited with their commodore. Marty, who was rehabilitated, told them what had happened up to then and informed them that the flotilla would return to base for a month.

"What I want you to do is carry on finding out what ships the Turks have in the Aegean and what the chances are of them sending reinforcements by sea," Marty said.

"When is the revolt planned to start?" Andrew asked.

"They planned it for next June," Marty said.

"I can hear a but." James frowned. Marty nodded.

"But, the plans were leaked so I am advising them to bring it forward to the end of winter. March preferably."

"What will we do?"

"Run interference and stop or delay any Ottoman reinforcements being delivered by sea."

"The marines?" Andrew asked.

"They can only advise unless directly attacked."

Hector chose that moment to get to know James. He sat beside him and stared directly at his eyes. James looked back. Hector raised a large paw and plonked it on his lap.

"Can I give him a treat?"

"If you want."

James took a biscuit and offered it to him. Hector very gently took it from his fingers then crunched and swallowed.

"He has his father's manners."

"And his mother's size. He is growing like a weed. I think he must weigh as much as Troy already." James laughed as Hector tried to climb on his lap.

"If those feet are anything to go by, he is going to grow a fair bit more yet," Andrew said.

Chapter 18: Lisbon

There was mail waiting when they got back to Zakynthos. One of Marty's letters was from James Turner. It instructed him, with all speed, to take the Eagle to Gibraltar and report to an address on Castle Steps. It was just two weeks old. *Why has he specified the Eagle? Because she's fast?* Whatever the reason he transferred himself and the Shadows and left immediately, leaving Wolfgang in charge of the flotilla.

The Eagle was a fast ship and was driven hard. They managed the trip in less than seven days. Marty walked with Hector up the twisty streets and knocked on the door of the address.

"Heard the Eagle had landed," James Turner quipped in greeting as he opened the door.

"Seven days, four hours. Might be a record," Marty replied.

"Impressive, pass my congratulations to Captain Archer."

They sat and were served coffee by a servant

"So, what is so urgent?"

"Insurrection."

"Well as I am already covering Greece, it must be somewhere else."

"Exactly, this one is in Portugal."

"What? The Portuguese don't revolt."

"They do now, the constitutionalists are up in arms."

Marty looked confused, "What the hell is a constitutionalist?"

"Simply put, it is a movement to put a formal constitution in place. They are following the movement in the two Sicilies that forced Ferdinand to sign one based on the Spanish constitution."

"What is the problem with that?"

"John opposes it. We want him to agree to it. He trusts you so I want you to go and talk to him."

"What about his wife?"

"He is the only one that matters, if she signs all well and good."

"I had better head to Lisbon then."

"Do you have clothes suitable for an ambassador?"

"Ambassador?"

"Didn't I mention that?"

"No, you omitted that small detail."

"You have been appointed Ambassador to Portugal for the duration of your stay. You have the facilities and staff at the embassy at your disposal."

"What does the incumbent think of that?"

"Thornton has had to return to England so there is only a Chargé d'affaires." James picked up a folder and handed it to Marty. "You will stay there until the new year."

"Caroline?"

"On her way. So you only need one suit to start with."

Marty gave James a sideways look as he opened the folder.

"Oh, by the way, you can stay here. More comfortable than the ship."

And less expensive than a hotel, no doubt.

Caroline boarded the Pride of Purbeck. Paul's children were sent to Dorset for Marty's family to care for. She had packed Marty's dinner suits and formal attire. He would be Viscount Stockley for the next few months. Edwin was at Rugby School and Constance was staying with the Armstrong family in Newmarket who were renowned horse breeders and trainers, where she could learn all she needed to set up her own stud.

At forty Caroline was still a strikingly beautiful woman. She had taken care of her figure by diet and exercise in the form of dance and fencing. She had no grey in her hair. She had brought her staff with her. Mary, Tabetha, Melissa and two footmen.

The captain, Victor Dunbar, was making sure all her luggage was stowed. "Do you want that case in your cabin?" he said pointing to a long narrow leather case.

"Those are my swords. I will fence with Melissa so yes please. I will have my gun case in my room as well. I can practise shooting as we sail."

The captain nodded and gave an order to a crewman. He was new to the post having been Captain of the Constance, one of the Stockley clipper fleet. He had heard that their lord and ladyship were martial in their habits and assumed this was normal as none of the crew bat an eyelid.

She had an old dog with her. It was a big shepherd of some type. Brindled like a mastiff but not as heavily built. Still, it looked like it could do someone some real damage if it wanted to. Despite its age it was fairly vigorous and never left her side.

Then there were her two footmen. They were obviously former military men from their bearing. Broad shouldered and fit looking they were watchful in a protective way rather than in the manner of servants. He was sure both of them were carrying weapons as he noted a bulge at the back of their belts under their coats.

He paid particular attention to her maids and the girl who had been introduced as her secretary. Mary was older, around the same age as him and a widow by all accounts. The other, a dark-skinned lass who had an exotic accent from the Caribbean, Jamaica if he wasn't mistaken, wore a wedding ring. Melissa, the secretary, was very pretty and around seventeen years old at a guess. Her ladyship treated her more like a daughter than an employee.

"All loaded, skipper," Edmonds, the first mate, reported.

"Get us out into the river," Dunbar growled.

Marty went to the best tailor in Gibraltar and had a suit made. It was a sombre black, made of fine wool cloth. Long tails, with swallow-tailed lapels, and high-waisted trousers. He also ordered three silk shirts, cravats, and stockings. That would keep him in Gibraltar for three more days.

James Turner used the time to bring him up to date on what was going on. "I suppose you want to know how Beth got on her first mission?"

"She survived so she can tell me herself when we return for the coronation," Marty said.

"She did, well suffice to say she didn't disgrace herself."

"What else is happening?"

"George Canning has completed the reorganisation of the Intelligence Service. It was a bit of a struggle and there was some resistance from the army."

"No surprise there. Did Arthur intervene?" Marty said, referring to the Duke of Wellington.

"He did, and a good job he did too."

"How is George?"

"The king," James said with an admonishing look, "is fat and frustrated. The bill he is trying to get through parliament is stalled and doesn't stand a chance of passing. His damn wife is back as well and stirring up the masses."

"She is active?"

"No, it's her very presence that causes a problem."

"She was in Italy, wasn't she?"

"Yes, and she should have stayed there with her lover. She wants to be active as Queen." James sighed.

"Can't see George agreeing to that. The man wants to be rid of her."

The days passed, and his suit was ready. He took his leave from James and the Eagle tore out of harbour as soon as he was aboard. The trip to Lisbon only took thirty hours.

The Pride cruised into the Port of Lisbon. There were a few British merchantmen and a couple of warships anchored in the Tagus and along the docks but no sign of any of the flotilla. Caroline stood at the rail and scanned the shore. Troy came up beside her, put his front paws on the rail and barked once.

Caroline looked in the same direction as he was and saw a carriage coming down the dock. It was an open landau, and she could see a man with a shock of black hair with a large brown dog sitting on the seat beside him.

The Pride swung around into the wind, coming to a halt a scant twelve feet from the dock. Messenger lines were thrown across and once the mooring cables were pulled over and fixed, she pulled herself in. The coach stopped opposite to where the gangway would be lowered.

Marty stepped down and looked up at her. His smile was wide enough to crack his face. Hector stepped up beside him and woofed at Troy. Troy, in a fit of excitement, hardly waited for the gangplank to touch down before he was across it and running in circles at Marty's feet. Hector joined in and soon Marty was on knees being licked and cuddled.

"When your dogs have finished, how about a kiss for your wife?" Caroline said.

Marty pushed the dogs away and stood. He took a handkerchief and wiped his face before taking her into his arms and kissing her deeply. The dogs bounded away playing chase and catching up in the backside sniffing stakes.

When they separated Caroline said, "That's better. Hello Mr Ambassador. Where is your ship?"

"Sent her back to the flotilla. She will carry messages back and forth."

"So, it's true. We are staying here until the new year."

"Absolutely, nothing will be happening in Greece before then."

A pair of wagons, drawn by large horses, and a second carriage pulled up.

"Two?" Caroline said, arching an eyebrow.

"I know my wife," Marty said and led her back onboard where he greeted the captain and the crew, thanking them all personally for taking care of his wife and her people.

The embassy was a large mansion set in the Rua de São Bernardo with its own large back garden. The union flag flew from a balcony on the first floor. It was fully staffed, and they were met at the door by the Chargé d'affaires, Edward Ward. He was thirty-one years old, and had married Lady Matilda Stewart in 1815. They had a son and a daughter three and two years old respectively.

"Lady Caroline, welcome," he said with an elegant bow.

"Mr Ward, I am pleased to meet you."

"Please call me Edward. Matilda is inside with the children."

They entered a large hallway with a desk, and a clerk was standing behind it.

"This is Josiah, he is our gatekeeper."

And so it continued until they entered their rooms where Matilda waited to greet them.

"Lady Caroline," she said.

"You can call me Caroline, if I can call you Matilda."

"I have read so much about you. It is wonderful to meet you."

"Half of what you read is fiction and the rest exaggerated." Caroline smiled.

Marty had been there two days already and had established a good relationship with Edward. He had made it very clear he was only there to guide the king and not to usurp his authority. Edward in turn appreciated Marty's honesty and candour.

Marty and Caroline visited Bemposta Palace at the invitation of King John who was King of the United Kingdom of Portugal, Brazil and the Algarves. His reign was a troubled one, with constant interference from foreign powers, invasion, and rebellion. There was currently a liberal revolt in Brazil led by his own son Pedro. His wife, Carlota, was Spanish and constantly undermined him by pushing Spanish interests ahead of Portugal's. He needed a friend.

They were greeted by the Duke of Cadaval, Nuno Caetano Álvares Pereira de Melo, Nuno to them. He led them to the throne room where the king and queen awaited them. Caroline laid her left hand on Marty's right as they walked towards the thrones. They advanced sedately which gave Marty time to observe the royals.

King John was heavily jowled, with a high forehead, grey hair and blue eyes. He was overweight and festooned in his honours. Queen Carlota was, in the kindest possible way, plain in her looks with a lantern jaw and shrewish set to her features. It was unusual for her to be present, as she had been caught conspiring against the King years before and had been effectively exiled to a remote palace. The surprising thing, given the couples antipathy, was that they had nine children. As they had just returned from Brazil, the current status of their relationship was unknown.

Marty and Caroline stopped and, as the duke introduced them, formally, Marty bowed and Caroline curtsied.

"Viscount Martin! Welcome!" King John said enthusiastically. "We have missed your presence. Lady Caroline you are as beautiful as the rumours say."

Queen Carlota's sour look turned to one of intense dislike. King John ignored her. Marty took note.

"Your Majesty, it is a pleasure to be here in Portugal again."

Carlota sneered at him. "And how many people will you kill this time?"

"Your Highness, the time before was one of treachery and deception by an enemy of Portugal. The business now is about mutual friendship," Marty said.

"My husband only kills if he has to, and then only enemies of our king and his allies," Caroline purred.

"Enough of that," King John said firmly, more to his wife than anyone else.

"Martin, would you walk with me? Ladies, please excuse us."

The king stood and led Marty back down the throne room and through the palace. As they walked, he said, "Forgive the queen for her rudeness. She hates everyone equally."

"She seems angry, your Majesty."

"She is always angry. Angry at my faith, angry at me, angry at the court. I do not think there is a single element of joy in her entire body. How we bred our children to be so handsome, I will never know. I can only put that down to the intervention of the almighty."

Marty let that go, "How may I be of assistance?"

"With her? Not at all. I only asked her here to see what her reaction to you and Lady Caroline would be."

Marty didn't understand that at all, and it must have shown.

"You see, we are faced with yet another crisis. I want to know if she is involved in it."

"Aah, so you were hoping that she and Caroline could, let's say, get along?"

"There was a chance."

Marty said nothing and just let them walk in comfortable silence. They reached the chapel which was as richly decorated as a cathedral.

"This is quite beautiful, isn't it?" the king said, looking up at the ceiling that was covered in biblical scenes. "It was built by Catherine in the late 17th and early 18th centuries. The chapel predates the rest of the palace by probably a hundred years. I worship here every day."

The king sighed and walked to the altar where he knelt and crossed himself while muttering a short prayer. Marty waited; he was not a catholic nor a devout Anglican come to that. The king rose and moved to a pew where he sat and beckoned Marty to sit beside him.

"My reign has been difficult. My mother was insane, my wife despises me, she had children because of duty, my people want to impose a constitution on me."

"A constitution is not a bad thing," Marty said. "Ferdinand seems to be managing quite well with the Spanish one."

"George doesn't have one."

"No, we have a set of laws that codify the workings of the state. That is even more restrictive. Cromwell saw to that." That was in his briefing.

"The queen opposes it and will never agree to it."

"Then that gives you the grounds to remove her power once and for all."

"I will think on your words," John said thoughtfully, a shrewd look in his eyes.

The king rose as did Marty and the two walked back to the throne room where they were immediately aware of a frosty silence.

So much for those two getting along.

Back at the embassy Marty sat with Edward and took the opportunity to introduce him to the Shadows.

"These are my team. Antton is the senior and Matai his deputy but having said that it is very much a team of equals all who have their own specialities. Suffice to say their skills cover pretty much any situation we find ourselves in."

"Intriguing, the note I received said you had been here before in a more clandestine roll."

"Yes, I was Wellington's Intelligence Officer, and the lads were with me. They are going to watch the queen to find out who she is talking to."

"You think she is involved in the constitutionalist movement?"

"Probably not as she is trying to persuade the king not to sign it. But then she is also convinced she would be a better ruler than him so we cannot discount her trying a double play."

Marty turned to the team. "For once we won't miss Billy as you don't need his muscles. I want to know who comes and goes from the Queluz Palace. If they talk to the queen in private and, if possible, what was said." The boys left.

"Is that all you need to tell them?" Edward said.

"Yes, they are very experienced agents."

Marty met with King John every day, even the weekends. The friendship that had started back in the war grew as did John's dependence on Marty's advice. That caused jealousy amongst the courtiers, and it wasn't long before an attempt was made on Marty's life.

He and Caroline were walking through Lisbon in the evening to go to the opera. Caroline loved them, especially the romantic ones, while Marty wasn't that bothered. He would rather watch a play as long as it was in English or French. This was Mozart's *The Magic Flute* and was in German. They were just passing the São Bento Palace on their way to the National Theatre when a group of thugs came out of the gardens and attacked them. They were armed with knives and clubs and probably expected to have an easy pair of targets.

How wrong could they be.

As soon as Marty sensed something was wrong, he raised his walking cane, held it in both hands, twisted the hilt and pulled the hidden twenty-four-inch blade free. Caroline's hands were already in the muff that hung in front of her, and they emerged with two short-barrelled, percussion-cap pistols with ivory hilts which she cocked with her thumbs.

The men burst out of the bushes that surrounded the palace gardens and charged them. Caroline fired her right pistol first and then the left when they were five paces away. Two men staggered and the other two came on. Marty met them with his sword in one hand and the stick/sheath on the other. He cracked the first man to reach him across the side of the head with the sheath as he spun away from the charge. That put him behind them, and he thrust his sword into the second one's kidney.

Caroline was not unarmed, she had dropped her muff pistols and reached through the hidden pockets in her dress to the silver-mounted daggers sheathed on her thighs that glinted in the moonlight as she drew them. The stunned man that Marty had hit staggered towards her. She spun, the blades held back hand and stabbed him first in the left side of his neck and then in the right with her other hand. She stepped back to avoid the spurt of blood from his severed carotid arteries.

Marty had finished off the second man with a thrust to the throat and turned to the two men that Caroline had shot. One was on the ground, unmoving, the other was clutching his stomach but still standing. Knowing he would need to talk to him later Marty knocked him unconscious with a sharp blow of the sword stick's pommel then treated his wound.

Soldiers appeared and after a short time were followed by an officer. Marty showed him a paper Edward had supplied that explained in Portuguese that he was a diplomat. The officer accepted it and signed they could go but insisted on taking the three bodies and the unconscious man to his barracks.

The next morning Marty went to see King John who when he heard they had been attacked angrily started giving orders to people in Portuguese. Marty had to move quickly to calm the angry king and get him to order the army to give him access to the bodies and the wounded man. Messengers were sent and an army officer turned up. It was King John's youngest son Miguel. The prince, who was heavily influenced by his mother, treated Marty with the minimum of politeness and was stiffly formal in his dealings with him.

Marty shrugged that off as he couldn't care one jot what the princeling thought of him. They arrived at a barracks, and he was taken to a shed where the corpses had been stored prior to burial. He searched the pockets, eliciting a badly-concealed exclamation from the prince. He found no money or anything else, they had been looted already. He asked to speak to the soldiers and officer that had been there the night before.

With the king's authority hanging over him the prince could not refuse, and the men were brought forward.

"Tell them that I want to see what was taken from the dead men's pockets."

The men looked at him blankly.

"Did you or your men search the dead men?" he asked the officer.

"Yes, he did," the prince translated.

"What did you find?"

"The usual stuff. Pocket knives, rubbish, money."

"How much money?"

The officer hesitated.

"I don't care if you keep it. I just want to know how much."

"Fifty reals."

"Where is the wounded man?"

"In the infirmary."

"Take me there."

The man was under guard, lying in a bed with a bandage around his middle. Marty was told by a doctor that the bullet had nicked his intestine but missed anything vital.

"Leave us alone with him," he told the doctor.

The man protested but the prince barked an order and he left. The guard kept his eyes to the front.

"Ask him who paid him."

The man refused to answer.

"You had fifty reals on you, that is more than the four of you would earn in a year. So, someone paid you to try and kill or wound me. Who was it?"

The man looked frightened.

"Someone who scares you. Well, I am infinitely scarier than whoever sent you to kill me."

Marty lent forward and placed his hand on the wound.

"Sir, you cannot," the prince said.

"Shut up and translate," Marty snarled and pressed down.

The man screamed.

Marty asked again.

"You are going to hang anyway so tell me."

He started to press down again when the man babbled.

"He says that he was paid by a man who approached him in the taverna. He hid his face, but he knew he was an aristo by his voice."

"How did he hide his face?"

"He had the hood of his cloak up."

"Did he see anything?"

"He had a beard, and his nose was scarred by the pox."

"Did you see his hands?"

The man thought for a moment. "Yes, he wore a ring on his right hand and his knuckles were gnarled like an old root."

"What did the ring look like?"

"Gold with a red stone. It had something engraved on it because it caught the candlelight."

"Which finger was it on?"

"His little finger."

Marty caught the faintest of breath intakes from Miguel during this line of questioning.

"Thank you for your cooperation. I will see if I can get them to commute your sentence to prison."

The man actually looked grateful.

"Why don't you want him hanged?" Miguel asked as they left the infirmary.

"He is a witness for one thing, and he was just trying to make a living. The one I want is the one who paid him. Does the description give you any ideas?"

Miguel shook his head. Marty thanked him, shook his hand and left for the palace. He walked down the street and round the corner. Once out of sight of the barracks gate he took off his coat and turned it inside out before putting it back on. He was now dressed in a pale blue overcoat rather than a black one. He took a hat out of his pocket and donned it.

He stepped out into the street and wandered over to a taverna. He chose a chair at a street side table and ordered coffee. He didn't have to wait long. Miguel left the barracks and headed at a fast walk towards the palace. Marty dropped a coin on the table, stood and followed him. He didn't have to worry about concealing that he was following him as Miguel didn't look back once.

Miguel knew he needed to warn João that the ambassador was on to him. He recognised him from the description the thug had given and was in fear for his friend's life. The ambassador's reputation was legendary. He had slaughtered hundreds, according to the stories he had heard in court, to help beat Napoleon, and even if they were exaggerated, was a renowned killer.

He entered the palace through a back entrance and went to João's office. He knocked and walked straight in. João de Sá Pereira Soares, Groom of the Stool, sat at his desk reading letters. He was the most powerful of the royal household and decided who got to talk to the king or not. His pockmarked face and goatee beard distinguished him as did the garnet set ring on his right little finger that was engraved with his seal.

"Miguel, what is it?"

"Did you pay some thugs to attack the British ambassador?"

"What? Why do you ask that?"

"Because one of them has just described you to him and if I recognise you from it, he will when he sees you."

João stroked his beard with a hand gnarled by arthritis.

"I heard he was attacked. So one survived did he?"

"Yes, he is in the infirmary under guard. Stockley is going to ask for him to be spared the rope in return for his cooperation."

"Is he indeed? That man is a nuisance and has far too much influence over the king."

"The king says he is a friend."

"He is a friend because his government tells him to be. The British want to control us."

Marty lent against the wall in the corridor and listened through the door. He didn't understand all of what was being said but the tone gave him some additional clues. He smiled and walked back outside, nodding to the guard as he left.

"Any luck?" Caroline asked when he plonked himself down in an armchair in their private drawing room.

"Yup, I know who sent them."

"Have you killed him?"

Marty laughed. "No, I haven't. He is too high up the food chain in the royal household to assassinate."

"He will try again then."

"Probably."

Caroline looked at him. He was planning something. She shrugged mentally; he would tell her when he was ready.

Chapter 19: Warning

Marty sat chatting with King John. They were comfortable in each other's company and had a mutual interest in dogs. Hector was privileged to be allowed into the royal apartment and lay at Marty's feet. The king's three Podengo hounds lay curled up around his chair. These were his favourites from the royal hunting pack and were two bitches and a dog. Hector hadn't reached puberty, so was not any more interested in the bitches than he was the dog. Conversely, they treated him like the puppy he was even if he was at least as big as any of them.

The servant left to get tea and the king said, "Have you met my Groom of the Stool?"

"Who? What does he do?"

"He is my right-hand man. The member of the household that is closest to me. Everyone else has to get past him to get to talk directly to me."

"You mean if there was somebody else as Ambassador, they would have to go through him?"

"Oh yes, it is only our past relationship that lets you bypass him."

The situation suddenly became clear, the man felt professionally slighted and that had hurt his pride enough to trigger the revenge attack. *I don't know, some people!*

The king summoned his groom who presented himself in mere minutes.

"João de Sá Pereira Soares, Groom of the Stool. This is Viscount Martin Stockley, the British ambassador and an old friend of mine." King John said.

There he was, pockmarked face, hooked nose, goatee beard, gnarled hands and a ring with a large garnet carved with a seal.

"Senhor Soares," Marty said as he stood and bowed just the right amount.

"Lord Stockley." The return bow was a fraction off, and he spoke very good English.

The king didn't notice and continued.

"You two are my most trusted advisors."

Marty would swear afterwards that he could hear Soares's teeth grinding at that.

"I have been asked by the Spanish to grant them access to Porto."

"What do they offer in return?" Soares said.

"They offer to pay for its use," the king replied.

Marty frowned, "Why do they need it? They have Cadiz and a deep-water port at Pontevedra."

"Does that matter?" the king asked.

"Yes, I think it does. When did they ask this?"

Soares looked sour faced and said, "Their ambassador asked a week ago."

"Strange that they would ask that after the revolution in Porto, don't you think?" Marty gave the king a second to absorb that then continued, "If they had a free route across Portuguese lands to Porto, they could chop off the top of the country like an egg. Of course, they would say they were trying to help quell a rebellion for you. By then you would have their troops all over that part of Portugal and the only way to get them out would be to go to war."

"You are a military man who only sees the world in military terms," Soares said.

"I am also a farmer, a father, and a merchant. I see the world in many ways." Marty smiled at him.

"You two have opposing views on the constitution as well."

"Britain has a constitutional monarchy and King George is a friend." Marty shrugged, "That gives me a particular view on things."

"We have always been an absolute monarchy and should always be so!" Soares snapped.

"Gentlemen, I have heard both sides of that argument here and in Brazil. My son Pedro is also a liberal."

Marty knew that at this time the king and his son had been discussing how to separate the Kingdom of Brazil from the Kingdom of Portugal. Added to that the liberal revolution in Porto was spreading south rapidly. It would only be a matter of time before it got to Lisbon as it was largely unopposed and one of their demands was to return Brazil to colonial status.

That night Marty and Caroline were due to attend a function thrown by the Russian embassy. They rode in a carriage to the embassy where they wined, dined, and danced the evening away. On the way back they heard a bang but neither paid much attention.

Laughing and dancing steps from the party they entered their living room to find Antton and Adam sat drinking a glass of something amber. Between them on the floor was a Portuguese man and propped up by the fireplace was a rifle.

"Evening, Boss," Antton said.

"You've been busy," Marty said and poured him and Caroline a drink. "Where did you find him?"

"On a roof that overlooked that well-lit section of street outside the theatre."

"How did you find him?" Caroline asked.

"It's the only well-lit bit of street on the route so it's where I would have set up," Adam said. "We checked the roofs and there he was."

"Is he alive?" Caroline asked as she prodded him with her toe.

"Just about. He struggled a lot and managed to fall off the roof."

"Have you questioned him?"

"No, he's been unconscious since then."

"Has Matai looked at him?" Marty said.

"He's on watch at the queen's palace."

Marty knelt by the man and ran his hands around his head and over his body.

"He's well and truly broken. I think he will die sooner rather than later. He has a lot of internal injuries.'

"Any idea who paid him? We found a purse with two hundred reals in it," Adam said.

"I have a very good idea. Bring him, we are going visiting."

Marty changed into a dark suit and the, now dead, man was wrapped in a blanket. Antton threw him over his shoulder, and they went to the stables where they saddled three horses. Marty led them out and rode a couple of miles to the outskirts of the city to the gates of a large house in extensive grounds. It started to rain as they dismounted and went through the gates on foot.

The drive was around three hundred yards long. The house, grand and dark. Marty didn't knock, he just used a set of picks to unlock the front door. He checked the hall and found the dining room.

"Put him there in the chair at the head of the table," he whispered.

Antton sat the body in the armed dining chair and arranged it to look like it was just sitting there. Marty took the pouch of reals and emptied them onto the table. He then took a note from his pocket he had written before they left and pinned it to the table with the man's dagger. They left as quietly as they had arrived leaving the front door open.

The next morning Soares was rudely awoken by a shrill scream. His bedroom door burst open a minute or so later and his butler rushed in ashen faced. Soares was sitting in bed in his nightgown with a nightcap on his head. His wife sat up beside him.

"My Lord, there is a dead man in the dining room."

Soares had a feeling of dread as he got out of bed and pulled on a robe. He pushed his feet into slippers and, with all the dignity he could muster, followed the butler downstairs. As he walked through the door he could see the man he had hired the day before sat at the end of the table. The man was a former member of the Portuguese rifle regiment and a crack shot. He had come highly recommended.

As he approached, he could see the man was dead, his face bloody. On the table in front of him was the money he had paid him. Stacked as if he had been counting it. In front of his outstretched right hand was a note pinned to the table with a dagger.

He walked to the end of the table ignoring the gasp from his wife behind him. He pulled out the dagger and picked up the note. It said in English:

This is your only warning.

He didn't need to ask who it was from.

Chapter 20: Smyrna

The Neaera was missing her boats. They had been left in Crete. She was now just an armed barque and took the place of the Eagle that was operating as a messenger. Angus had found her to be a good sailor and acting First Lieutenant James Stockley was taken with her guns and had plans for the future. He was convinced that exploding shell guns would change the course of naval warfare in the years to come. As it was, he had to make do with the variety of shot available to a gunner in the 1820s.

Their mission was to sail between the Turkish port of Smyrna and the coast of Greece to intercept any Ottoman reinforcements. Flying under the Greek flag, there should be no connection with the British. They had a lot of sea to cover so concentrated on the east coast of the mainland. As per their standard modus operandi they spread out in line to cover as much sea as possible.

James had the watch with the Neaera out on the eastern end of the line. They were cruising northeast at a casual five knots, the sun was shining but there was a line of dark cloud to the north.

"That storm ain't getting any closer," Jebediah said.

"I noticed," James said.

"Do you think we will see any Turkish troop ships?"

"If we do, they won't be alone. If I were them, I would send them in convoy with warships."

"What ships do they have?"

"Warships? Everything up to first rates of a hundred guns or more. They bought up a lot of surplus ships when the French and British downsized their navies."

"So, we could be going up against former navy ships?" Jebediah said with a hint of worry.

"Could be, but not sailed by our Jacks or commanded by British or French officers."

"Oh, that's alright then," Jebediah said sarcastically.

James smiled. If they found a convoy the chances were it would be lightly escorted as there hadn't been any trouble, up to now, in getting them across the Aegean. Their job was made easier as the Turks only had one strategic port on their west coast, Smyrna, which lay in a sheltered gulf.

They had been patrolling back and forth for several weeks when Captain Ackermann called an all-officers' meeting. Angus and James were rowed across to the Unicorn which was anchored a half cable away from them in the lee of the island of Psara. They went aboard and met Archer of the Eagle with Midshipman Sykes in tow.

"Evening, Trevor. All good?" Angus said.

"Bored of sailing up and down. I'm hoping that Wolfgang has had an idea."

They went down into Captain Ackermann's cabin and found that Lieutenants McGivern, Longstaff, Farrell and Brazier as well as the Unicorn's Sailing Master, Arnold Grey, were already in attendance.

"Welcome, gentlemen, take a coffee and a seat," Wolfgang said.

When they were all seated and paying attention he continued. "We have been patrolling for several weeks now and I can understand if you are bored and frustrated by it. Well, I am as well so we will try something else. Now, as you all know, the only port on this coast that the Ottomans use for anything, apart from Constantinople, is Smyrna. We have been patrolling off it for three weeks now."

Angus mocked a yawn.

"Precisely, now I want us to have a look inside."

"Who gets to go?" Trevor said.

"The Eagle, she can pass for an American and you have a set of papers to back it up. Change her name to match."

"From now on she is the Delaware," Trevor said.

James was disappointed, he had hoped for a moment that the Neaera would be chosen.

Wolfgang wasn't finished. "The Neaera will also enter the gulf and map any fortifications or defences. As you are so distinctive you had better go in under a Greek flag."

Arnold Grey looked up. "The city is mostly Greek but under Ottoman control. I stopped here once and was surprised that almost all the merchants spoke Greek."

"I thought everything on this side was Turkish," Trevor said.

"At one time the whole lot belonged to the Greeks," Simon said. "Until the Ottoman Empire spread, that is."

"Then the Neaera is to avoid contact with any ships as none of you speak modern Greek," Wolfgang said.

"What if we find that the harbour is full of troop ships?" Trevor said.

"Then there will be an unexpected fire in the middle of the night." Wolfgang grinned. "They are always tied up tight to each other."

The Eagle, now the Baltimore, sailed into the Gulf of Smyrna with the American flag flying proudly from her stern. Trevor Archer was on deck, most of the crew were below.

There was quite some traffic in the gulf which gave witness to how busy the port must be. The entrance to the gulf was some eleven miles wide and the waters were deep. It angled down to the southeast. For once the traffic seemed organised with everyone sticking to their channel. Theirs was on the north side.

He had no more than the usual lookouts a merchantman would have, and his carronades were covered and made to look like deck cargo. His intention was to sail down to the port, anchor, take his time looking around, and sail out. As they were about to enter the inlet to the port, he saw a flag run up the mast of the ship ahead of him. His heart sank as he recognised it.

"Send up the pilot flag and reduce sail to minimum steerage way."

Having a pilot onboard was the last thing he wanted, and he looked around the deck checking that everything was in order.

The armourer had been sharpening some weapons earlier and the wheel was still on deck.

"Get that sharpening wheel below along with any weapons."

Two men rushed to move it as the flag went up the halyard.

Midshipman Sykes came on deck dressed as the first mate.

"What's afoot, skipper?" he asked with a fairly good imitation of an American accent.

"Very good! Wasted on the Greeks though," Trevor laughed then sobered. "They will be putting a pilot aboard."

"I'll check the deck."

It's time he made Lieutenant.

On the Neaera, Marty and Hamish were busy observing the coast and making notes on the chart as they rounded the headland to enter the gulf.

"According to the chart, there is a castle in the town of Foça. It looks like it is called The Castle of the Five Gates."

They went between Orak Adasi Island and the coast, then had to swing out around another island and a headland after which a large bay opened up. The castle was clearly visible on a promontory.

"Doesn't look occupied, let alone armed," Hamish said.

"No guns visible, no flags. I can see the gates. Look, someone is opening one."

They both focussed their telescopes on the men opening the second gate.

"What are they doing?" James said as four went inside.

Moments later the bow of a fishing boat appeared. It was moving smoothly and soon they saw how. It was mounted on a two-wheeled carriage.

"They are using it as a boat shed," Hamish said as the boat came fully out, and they could see the four men were at the back pushing it.

"Let's go down this side then back up the other."

They continued on down to the inlet which led to the town. They found nothing.

"Trevor is reconnoitring the town so we will go up the other side of the gulf and see what we find."

Trevor hove to while the pilot boarded. The man spoke very bad English but made himself understood. He navigated them into port and had them tie-up beside a Swedish barque. Even though it was late November it was warm, and the men below would be getting hot.

"I want you to rotate the men on deck with those below, so they all get some air and set up sails to direct the breeze below."

"Aye, aye, Skipper."

He looked around the harbour then pantomimed that he had seen something in the rigging. The view from the top gallant yard was much better and he could see into the military part of the harbour. In it were a number of warships; two forty-gun frigates, a thirty-six-gun frigate, a seventy-four, and a hundred-gun first rate. Tied up in a group were four briggs, two flutes and two xebecs. Pretending to finish fixing whatever he was supposed to have seen from the deck he descended to find the captain of the Swedish ship leaning on the rail and watching him.

"Interesting ship you have there," the Swede said.

"She's my pride and joy," Trevor replied amiably.

"You have big guns for a merchant."

"I'm Trevor Archer, Captain of the Baltimore out of Boston and you are?"

"Sven Nilsson, Captain of the Mina out of Malmo."

"Pleased to meet you, Captain."

The Swede laughed heartily. "Call me Sven. What are you carrying?"

"The usual, tobacco and sugar. I thought we would come here and check the prices."

"Good luck with that. The Greeks bargain like gypsies."

Trevor looked disappointed. "Well if they aren't good enough, I'll take my cargo somewhere else."

"The best prices for your goods will be in France. Try Marseille or Toulon. Now tell me about those guns."

"Carronades, they weigh half of what a cannon does and pack a good punch. Not only that, it only takes three men to man them. I can carry the same firepower for half the weight so can carry more cargo. Great against pirates."

"Now that is a thought, there are still some freebooters around. Would be nice to give them a surprise. Why don't you come over and have a drink with me this evening?"

"I was planning on eating ashore. Why don't you join me, and we can get drunk and tell stories."

Again, the hearty laugh. "That sounds like a very good idea, my friend."

Marine Corporal Norman Read was perched on the top gallant yard with a drawing board, paper and pencils. He sat next to the lookout and sketched items of interest while the Eagle sailed, almost casually, out of the harbour. Norman had joined the marines as a seventeen-year-old after he was caught in flagrante delicto with the sixteen-year-old daughter of the local butcher in his hometown of Rayleigh in Essex. The butcher, understandably, was somewhat upset by what he saw as the violation of his little princess. The fact was, the minx had seduced him and there ended his plans to become an artist. He fled to Chatham and took the king's shilling.

Now here he was ten years later practising his art by sketching hills and bays. Gregory Marsh, the lookout, had the sharpest eyes on the ship and was scanning the island as they passed it.

"'ere, Norm, there's something on that hill over there." Greg pointed to a hill on the end of a small peninsula.

"Can you see what it is?"

Gregory swung the glass he had hung over his shoulder around and took a closer look.

"Battery, six guns. Can't tell what they are yet. Turkish flag flying above them."

"Let me see."

Norman took the glass and focussed it on the hill. "Six guns alright. Set to cover the passage."

There was a glint of light from the hill.

"They are watching us." Norman quickly sketched what he had seen then made a more detailed drawing of the peninsula.

They were now level with the battery, and he could see it clearly with the naked eye.

Norman was sketching furiously and when he had finished took a stay to the deck.

The flotilla reassembled and headed to the rendezvous point with the Endellion. She arrived a day late. Wolfgang called his captains together and asked Norman to join them to brief Phillip Trenchard.

"From our reconnaissance of the Gulf of Smyrna and the port, we have established that there is only one defensive position guarding the approach to the city and port and that is on a peninsula just inside the inlet. Corporal Read, tell the captain what you saw," Trevor Archer said.

Norman placed his sketches on the table. He had filled in details with watercolours.

"The battery is on this hill on the end of the peninsula. With it they control access to the city. It has six twenty-four-pound-cannon behind caissons. From what we could see the fortification also houses at least a platoon of infantry as well as the gunners."

"This peninsula is where?" Wolfgang said, looking at a large-scale chart.

"There." Norman pointed to the place on the chart. With their elevated position they can reach any ship passing through the inlet."

Wolfgang turned to James and Hamish. "You didn't find any other defences?"

"Not a thing. Even the castle at the mouth of the gulf is inactive and being used as a boatshed."

"Trevor, what did you find in the harbour?" Wolfgang asked.

"Warships, and eight ships in ordinary, tied up in a group."

"That's interesting, why keep eight ships in ordinary?" Andrew Stamp asked.

"They could be troop ships," Trevor said.

"Was there a large garrison in the town?" Wolfgang asked.

"There is a castle. Here," Trevor said, pointing to a point on the edge of the town, "and there are a lot of soldiers. I had dinner with a Swedish skipper, and he said he had seen a steady increase in the number of troops over the last month."

"Why has he been in port for that long?"

"A couple of reasons, he is selling Stockholm tar, is determined to get the best price no matter how long it takes and he wants a high-value cargo to take back and is waiting for a shipment of saffron to add to a cargo of marble."

Wolfgang turned to Phillip and passed him a package. "This is the written report along with copies of all the drawings for Lord Martin. Get it to him as soon as you can."

Chapter 21: Constitution

December came and the demands of the revolution got louder and in proportion, the queen's determination to oust the king and keep the absolutist monarchy in place increased. Marty had had no more attempts on his life and Soares was keeping out of his way. The Shadows had established that Soares visited the queen at least twice every week. Marty had persuaded the king to implant a spy in her household.

Caroline disliked the queen intensely which made it difficult for her if the woman was in the same room. Fortunately, the occasions when that happened were getting rarer as the king distanced himself from his wife.

The liberals formed a parliament and set in process complicated elections based on the Spanish system. Every man over the age of twenty-five, and some men of twenty-one, were permitted to vote if they had a job or trade or useful occupation. They voted to elect members of an electoral college who would then elect the members of parliament. It worked out that there was a member for every thirty thousand inhabitants. That parliament had come up with a constitutional document that they wanted the king and queen to sign. The king had negotiated on it but was putting off signing it which was upsetting the masses.

The Eagle docked and Trevor went straight to the embassy.

"Trevor, welcome. Is that the report on Smyrna?" Marty said as Trevor sat.

"It is." Trevor replied and handed the package over. He knew that Marty would want a verbal summary and continued. "The port is relatively undefended apart from one battery at the entrance to the inlet. The naval docks are marked on the chart in the package and contain a group of ships, in ordinary, that could be troop ships."

"Interesting, how are they moored?"

"In a group, hull to hull."

"They will have to be rendered unusable just before the uprising, which, by the way, will start next month. So, I want those ships out of the picture by the fifteenth of January. In the meantime, the flotilla should celebrate Christmas. I have arranged for special supplies to be provided and they are being shipped to the dock for loading on the Endellion."

"That's very kind of you, Milord."

"I would really like to be there with you, but I have to stay here until the king signs the constitution. I want you to return here as soon as those ships are destroyed. Hopefully I will be free to join the flotilla then."

The waiting chaffed on Marty. He was at the core of his being a man of action not a diplomat. Caroline knew that and tried to distract him with preparations for the festive season. The embassy was decked out with paper chains and boughs of pine. Holly was only available in the north but she had found ivy for wreaths.

The king was dragging his feet over signing the constitution and the people were getting impatient. A mob had the palace under siege. Marty decided it was now or never.

"Take me to the palace," he told the coachman. The Shadows were mounted and formed up around him.

The streets were full of protestors and the Shadows cleared a path gently but firmly, exhibiting superb horsemanship. Antton led and danced his horse sideways to push some men aside. A man reached up and grabbed his leg. He looked down and the man saw his death in eyes that were as cold as ice and backed away.

They reached the palace gates. A platoon of soldiers came out, formed up and made a path. Marty's coach serenely entered the palace grounds followed by his men.

"I'm here to see the king. Where is he?" he said in Portuguese to the first palace flunky he saw.

"In the gardens, Sir."

Marty walked around the palace to the large ornamental garden at the rear. Adam, Antton and Matai followed. Finding the king was not difficult, he was surrounded by a mass of courtiers and servants and the babble of conversation could be heard a long way away.

Marty signalled for the boys to hang back and made his way through to the middle of the huddle. A very attractive woman flashed her eyes at him, her fan in her left hand held in front of her face in the signal for wanting to get to know him. He ignored it and stepped into the clear area around where King John was sat on a garden bench.

"Martin, this is a surprise. The weather is so unseasonably warm, I couldn't resist moving the court out here."

"Your Majesty. The mob is at the gates. You need to sign or risk civil war."

"As always, straight to the point," the king sighed.

Marty moved into, what was in public, an indecent range so he could say quietly for the king's ears only. "John, you are playing into your wife's hands. The longer you wait, the stronger she becomes."

That got the king's attention and he stood. "You are all dismissed. Martin, stay." He turned to a servant, "Go and fetch the royal clerk, tell him to bring that damnable constitutional document." A sentry was next. "Go to the officer at the gates and have him bring the leader of the parliament. He is not to arrest him but to invite him."

The Duke of Cavadal was stood some way off and the king sent a servant to fetch him. "You will be a witness," he said to the confused-looking aristocrat.

Marty ignored the fact that the king had commanded him rather than asked. The situation was delicate, and he needed to handle it carefully.

"Should I sign this?" the king asked, holding up the document in front of Marty.

"Your Majesty, the future of the monarchy is in your hands. Sign it or set the army on your own people to restore order," Marty said bluntly.

The duke gasped. One didn't talk to the king like that. He was about to admonish Marty when the king reacted.

"You would advocate I kill my own people?"

"Not at all, I simply put the alternatives to you."

"I see why George values your friendship."

An infantry captain approached with a man in tow. He spoke to him in Portuguese, the duke muttered a translation for Marty.

"The king asks where they want to see the Bases of the Constitution document signed. The politico is saying they just need his approval of this document to go ahead and draft the full constitution. The king asks when that will be ready, and he says that it will be completed sometime in June."

The king asked the clerk for a pen and ink and signed the document there and then. The clerk then attached the royal seal.

"The politico is asking if the queen will sign. The king says she will not. The politico asks if the king wants to detach the queen from all political and royal activities. The king says yes."

Well that solves that problem.

With the king's approval obtained, the mob dispersed and Marty returned to the embassy. Christmas could be enjoyed, and he could return to the flotilla in the new year.

Caroline had a surprise for him. The Neaera was in port and James was waiting for him in his study.

"Hello, son." Marty embraced him. "What's the Neaera doing here?"

"Wolfgang thought you would want to be there when we attack the port and the Neaera is more comfortable than the Endellion."

"And almost as fast," Marty laughed. "We will leave on the second."

"Is your business with the king completed?"

"Let's say it is moving in the right direction. The packet delivered mail yesterday."

"Anything from Beth?"

"Yes, she is going to Russia."

"Russia? What is going on there?"

"No idea, but they are always up to something."

James glanced at the door.

"Melissa is with your mother at this time of day. You will have to wait until she has completed her work."

James blushed.

"You will have her company for three weeks before we leave. You can wait for an hour or so."

They sat in companionable silence for a while. Marty knew his son had something on his mind so wasn't surprised when James said, "Father."

"Yes."

"How old were you when you married mother?"

"Too young, twenty years old."

"Oh."

"You are thinking of asking Melissa to marry you?"

"We would like to."

Marty noted the use of 'we'.

"So, you have already talked to her about it. Does your mother know?"

"Mother?" James looked worried. "No, I don't think so."

"Well, you will have to ask her as she is Melissa's legal guardian. You will also need my consent as you are still under twenty-one."

"Did your father give his consent?"

"No, Pop had been dead for several years by then and Mum was there when I asked her."

"She approved then?"

"Oh yes, why wouldn't she? Caroline was a lady, wealthy, beautiful, and pregnant."

James coughed as the sip of tea he was taking went down the wrong way.

"Pregnant? With Beth?"

"Yes, we had to get the marriage done before she showed too much."

James was flummoxed. This had never been discussed in front of them.

"You and mother were—"

"Lovers before we became husband and wife."

James blushed again and looked shocked.

"You youngsters didn't invent love. I fell in love with your mother the first time she whispered in my ear. Which was also the first time I saw her."

The blush was replaced with a calculating look.

"Don't even think about it," Marty said. "Not in this house."

"Oh, I would never do anything to embarrass you or mother," James said, the picture of innocence.

"He wants to marry Melissa. That's no surprise," Caroline said after Marty gave her a heavily-edited version of his conversation with James.

"I told him about our wedding."

Caroline looked at him directly. "That I was pregnant?"

"Yes. He is old enough to know that now."

"So is Beth, but she worked it out for herself."

That was news to Marty. He had no idea that her daughter knew she was a honeymoon baby.

"Does he want to follow in your footsteps?" Caroline asked.

"You mean to be lovers first?"

Caroline just gave him the 'don't be stupid' look.

"He's thinking about it."

"So is she, she asked me about how to protect herself against getting pregnant."

"It's just a matter of time then."

Later that night, well after midnight, a floorboard creaked. Caroline, awake despite the hour, heard it and smiled. Marty slept on, oblivious.

Christmas Eve came. The embassy was full of Christmas cheer. Hamish had joined them from the Neaera, and the crew were given shore leave. During the day the embassy children were given their presents. The servants had the day off and Rolland and the Shadows prepared lunch. Melissa and James were inseparable and were never more than a touch apart.

At midnight the adults attended mass at St George's church. Marty was glad to see many of the Neaera's crew there. Hamish attended as well as there was no presbyterian church in Lisbon. His dour demeanour was slightly disapproving of the more celebratory nature of the service, but he endured.

Christmas day started late. They attended church then had a sumptuous lunch featuring Marty's favourite, the five-bird roast, roast beef and a baked ham. The five-bird roast was turkey breast butterflied and layered with pheasant, chicken, duck, pigeon and pork sausage meat. The afternoon was spent playing parlour games or sleeping off lunch. That evening the embassy was holding a ball in the Ajuda palace as the embassy didn't have a ballroom that was big enough.

A chamber orchestra played in the gallery. The ceiling was divided into seven panels hung with crystal chandeliers. A newly-painted landscape of the king returning from Brazil adorned one wall. The rest were covered in red silk and mirrors. A buffet was provided in an anteroom and, of course, servants circulated with trays of wine.

King John attended, the queen did not. Despite his girth he turned out to be a very good dancer and whirled Caroline around the dancefloor more than once. Melissa and James had eyes for no one but each other. Marty danced with a different woman every dance. Caroline teased him that he left a trail of broken toes behind him, which wasn't true as he was a fine dancer. Hamish surprised everyone by whirling the wife of the Bavarian ambassador around the floor in a wild polka that left all the participants laughing and gasping for breath.

All in all, the ball was a success. Boxing Day was for recovery and letting the servants celebrate. The food that was left over would be donated to the church to give to the poor.

Caroline surprised Marty when she presented him with a rosewood case. In it were a pair of pistols the like of which he had never seen before. Made by Francotte in Belgium, they were revolving chamber repeating pistols. A hammer action fired .43 calibre pinfire cartridges through a six-inch hexagonal barrel. The frame was delightfully engraved, the trigger enclosed in a slim trigger guard.

"Where on earth did you find these?" Marty said.

"I had my agents around Europe keep an eye on the more innovative gunsmiths and they came up with these just in time to get a pair for Christmas." Caroline smiled. "Melissa got a pair for James as well."

"I will have to get holsters made," Marty said.

Caroline reached behind her chair and pulled out a second present.

"You didn't!"

"You will be leaving soon so I had them made."

The present contained a harness that had two holsters that were sprung to hold the pistols in place and pouches to hold a reload for each pistol. Marty took off his jacket and slipped the harness on, buttoning the ends to specially-fitted buttons on his trousers. He slipped the guns into the holsters and put his jacket back on.

"They don't show." Caroline smiled. "Just remember to leave a cylinder empty to avoid shooting yourself by accident."

"That still gives me four shots from each gun. They double my firepower during boardings."

Caroline sat on his lap and kissed him. "Anything that keeps you safe."

Chapter 22: Revolution

Marty and the Shadows re-joined the Unicorn in time to take over the raid on Smyrna. He briefed his men and Wolfgang, "This operation has to be carried out quietly and the fire has to look like an accident. I have given it a lot of thought and the Shadows and I will carry it out. We will go ashore to the west of the town after dark and return before dawn."

"How will you get ashore?" Wolfgang asked.

"You can sail us to just outside of the inlet and we will use the longboat to sail in from there. The battery will probably think it is a fishing boat if they spot it at all."

"Why not sail right into the harbour?"

"The ships are in the military part and, according to Trevor's report, docked at the end of a wooden pier. A fishing boat sailing into that area will be challenged by the guard boats. We can make our way through the town to the pier."

The plan was put into operation. The Unicorn sailed down the gulf in the late afternoon and hove to just to the north of the inlet after dark. It was a cloudy night, the moon filtering through a layer of high, thin clouds when it wasn't obscured by lower heavy ones.

The long boat had a mast stepped and a sail similar to a local fishing boat set. It was crewed by the Shadows and Marty was the last to step down into it. They were dressed as Turks. They sailed down the inlet, staying to the middle, following the lights of the town. They went ashore in a bay three miles west of the town that was bordered with orange groves. The boat was secured, and they set out along a dirt road that headed in the right direction.

The only buildings were isolated stone farmhouses until they got to the outskirts of the town. It was midnight and most of the houses were dark. They split up into pairs to make themselves less conspicuous. Smyrna was not a big town for all its importance as a port. The western end was predominantly Turkish and the eastern Greek. The harbour sat somewhere in the middle and was surrounded by businesses that were predominantly run by Greeks.

They avoided contact with any people out on the streets, especially the night watch. The watchmen were easy to spot as they carried lanterns on a pole. Marty smiled; they were making it easy for them. They reached the harbour and regrouped. There was a single guard sat on a crate at the entrance to the dock.

Chin and Adam walked past him and started pushing each other and swearing. The pushing turned into a wrestling match. The guard watched them for a while then stood and walked over to them as they went to ground. He prodded the nearest body with the butt of his pike and shouted at them.

Marty and the rest of the team slipped silently onto the dock and made their way to the end. The ships weren't moored directly to the dock but around thirty feet off the end. Marty stepped aside and Antton stepped up to the edge pulling a folded grapnel out of his pack. There was a click as he pulled out the tines. He whirled it around on the end of a line and launched it. The hook caught in the ratlines and they pulled the line tight, making it fast to a bollard. Antton was first across.

Marty, Antton, Garai and Matai searched the ship. It was empty so they moved onto the next. They were all empty apart from the third where they found a watchkeeper who was dispatched as he slept. Marty decided that the fire should start right there in his cabin. Combustibles were gathered from around the ship including a barrel of Stockholm tar that they found in a stack on deck. A timer on a pile of priming powder would start the fire. The stack of tar barrels was moved to be directly above the cabin.

Matai had moved across to check the other ships. They all had barrels of tar stacked on the decks.

"They must be getting ready to prepare them for sea. One of the other ships has fresh rigging coiled on deck and there is a stack of timber on the end one."

"We are just in time then, let's get out of here," Marty said.

They exited the same way they came, undid the rope from the bollard and let it drop into the sea. The guard had returned to his crate at the end of the pier. Marty crept up behind him a blackjack in his hand. He stopped just short of him as he heard a soft snore.

They were almost back to their boat when bells started to ring in the town. An orange glow could be seen reflecting from the low cloud and illuminated a column of smoke. The sound of a dull whump reached them and flames could be seen snaking skywards as a barrel of tar went off like a rocket.

The flotilla left the Gulf of Smyrna behind them and set course for the coast of Greece with the intention of collecting the marines. They got halfway when a storm came in from the northwest and the temperature plummeted. The wind swung to the northwest and the barometer dropped dramatically.

"What the hell is going on?" Marty asked Arnold Grey as rain turned to sleet.

"Looks to me like this moved down from the north. It has brought cold air and rain with it. We will have to run southeast." Arnold moved into the chart room. "We can probably shelter in the lee of Ikeria Island."

"Damn that's not what I wanted. There's a big meeting of the church and chieftains in Vostitsa. Papaflessas is going to represent the Feliki's plans to start the revolution."

"When is it?"

"On the 26th."

"Well it's the 16th today. If this blows over in the next few days, we can make it easily."

It didn't blow over in a few days. They were unable to make Ikeria and were blown southeast. The crews constantly changing sail settings and pumping as the ships worked.

James was on watch on the Neaera. It was the middle of the day but it was almost like dusk. The sun was obscured by heavy grey clouds and the sleet was slanting down. His oilskins provided only minimal protection and the towel he had wrapped around his neck to stop the ice-cold sleet from dripping down his neck was already saturated. There was a blinding flash and a deck-shuddering bang, as lightning struck the sea a hundred yards to port. He blinked and could see the afterimage on the inside of his eyelids.

"Fuck, that was close."

"Sir?" said Conner O'Doul, the helmsman closest to him. There were two on the wheel.

"Nothing. Watch your heading. Do not lose the Unicorn."

His vision cleared just as the lookout hailed, "Deck there! Squall coming in on the port quarter."

James spun and ran to the rail. He could see it heading right at him.

"Hard to starboard!"

The wheel spun as the helmsmen turned it for all they were worth. And the bow slowly swung. It was too little too late and the squall hit the port quarter hard. The triple reefed spanker blew out with a bang. Ripped from top to bottom.

"Get the mizzen crew up to get that replaced!" he shouted at a mate who disappeared below to reappear with the mizzen division. The flapping canvas was wrestled down and a new sail brought up from below. It was rigged fore and aft so it was easier to replace than some.

"Get us back behind the Unicorn."

Then the sleet turned to snow. Big wet flakes that melted as they touched down. It was no less wet and even colder. James was miserable.

A blue flare went up from the Unicorn followed by a white one.

"Prepare to turn to port. All hands to the sails. Tell the captain that we are changing course." A boy ran below.

Angus came on deck.

"Where are we?" he asked.

"Somewhere in the Dodecanese islands, I think. The Unicorn is turning, probably to get behind one of them."

"Deck there! Land two points off the port bow!" the lookout bellowed.

"I think you are right."

The ship rolled and pitched as they turned across the line of the waves. She corkscrewed horribly. Then, as they passed the headland it calmed, and the wind dropped a little. They had rounded the southern tip of Kos. The Unicorn led them northeast to the bay of Kefalos and anchored.

"Bring her up into the wind and ready the best bower anchor," Angus ordered.

The ship swung and slowed to a halt. "Anchor away!" James called.

"Back her up a cable and a half then drop a stern anchor," Angus said.

"Aye Aye, Captain." James smiled glad to not have to fight to keep his feet.

The rear anchor was dropped then the men at the capstan marched around to pull in the forward cable until the ship sat between the two.

"Secure all sails."

The Neaera soon sat as tidily as if she was in Chatham harbour. James went below and shed his wet clothes and briskly rubbed himself down with a towel. It was marginally warmer in his cabin than on deck and a whole lot drier. He went to his footlocker and pulled out a shirt, trousers, socks and a woollen argyle jumper his mother had given him. He pulled on hessian boots and felt warm for the first time in hours.

There was a knock at the door.

"Yes."

"Captain's compliments, your presence is required on the Unicorn," Jack Wilson his steward said.

Damn. He stepped outside and pulled on his oilskin coat and hat.

"There's a boat waiting alongside, Sir."

Dennis was waiting for him on deck with Archie, his dog. James couldn't go anywhere without either of them. Dennis was a big man with the mind of a seven-year-old, what would be called in later years Down's syndrome but was called mongolism in those days. James was his hero, surrogate father, and protector. Archie was a half-grown Dutch shepherd/Irish setter cross and a bundle of mindless energy. Oh, he had the smarts of his shepherd side when he wanted to use them, but the brainless Irish setter side would dominate if there was any fun to be had.

Dennis preceded him into the boat with Archie on his shoulders. The dog, quite happy and trusting the big man implicitly. James was last in and surprised that Angus wasn't coming along. They were only a half cable from the Unicorn so it was a relatively short and not too damp trip. He was first up the side as was his right.

He was met by Eric Longstaff who laughed when Archie appeared at the port on Dennis's shoulders. A woof from the quarterdeck was greeted by an enthusiastic reply and Dennis just about put him down in time before he jumped. Archie and Hector were soon entertaining the crew by chasing each other in a madcap race around the deck.

"The commodore is waiting in his cabin for you," Eric finally managed to say between laughs.

Marty was reading a book when the sentry announced that James had arrived. He already knew of course as the thunder of paws on the deck above his head and the calls of the crew had already announced that James and Archie were aboard.

"Hello, Father."

"Good evening, James, is Dennis looking out for the dogs?"

"He is, for some reason they respond really well to him."

"How is his training coming along?"

"Very well. He has learnt all the commands and is attentive when he knows we are working. His Irish setter heritage comes out when he plays."

There was a rumble of paws overhead as the dogs chased one another around the quarterdeck.

"How is Hector coming along?"

"His father's intelligence and his mother's strength and size. He learns fast, is very protective, loyal and, dare I say, cuddly."

James laughed. "You should never have allowed him on your lap when he was small. Mother did mention it once or twice. How much does he weigh now?"

"Around sixty pounds, and at a year old he has at least two more to grow."

"You are going to have to break him of the habit."

"I know. You will sit your Lieutenant's Board when we return to England along with Donaldson, Sykes, and Williams," Marty said in a sudden change of subject.

James wasn't fazed, he was used to his father's mercurial shifts.

"I know, I am ready as I am sure they are."

"You will have the opportunity to take a position on a new ship."

"I'm content where I am. Is this why you called me over?"

Marty sat back. "Partly. You have a long career ahead of you."

"And many things will change in the coming years. Steam will come and who knows how that will change the way the navy runs."

"As long as you know your own mind."

"Don't worry, Pop, I will be alright."

Marty smiled at the use of the familiarism that he had used for his grandfather.

"Will you join me for dinner?"

"Of course, I wouldn't miss one of Roland's creations."

The two had a companionable evening before James returned to the Neaera, reacquainting with his father after all the running around had been a treat. As Wolfgang said later, "Some quality father and son time. Needed by both."

It was the end of January, moving into February before the weather allowed them to make sail to the northwest or even leave the bay. Marty was keen to get his men back and to find out what the outcome of the gathering had been, so they made all speed to Paralio Astros.

The marines under Declan were waiting for them. Marty met with Papaflessas.

"How did the gathering go? I am sorry I couldn't be there, but a storm trapped us in the islands to the south."

"They wanted guarantees that the Russians would aid us. The Russians will supply arms but no military assistance."

"Does that mean the revolution will not start?"

"Not at all. Bishop Germanos will declare war on behalf of the Maniots next month. The armies of Mavromichalis and Kolokotronis will converge on Kalamata and it will begin. We thank you for your help. The training has been invaluable."

"You are more than welcome. I will direct my agent to send false information to the Ottomans that the attack will come in June and on Patras."

"That will also help. If you can confuse them, all the better."

Marty shook his hand, "I believe we have fulfilled our part of the bargain."

"You more than have and we will fulfil ours once we have our country and islands back." The Endellion was dispatched with instructions for Veronica and Billy. The flotilla left to go to Vostitsa where they were told the marines under Paul would be waiting. It took two days with favourable winds. The marines were recovered, and Marty met Paul and General Androutsos who had become firm friends.

"We are ready as we are going to be," Paul said.

"We?" Marty replied with an enquiring look.

"I am staying for at least the first part of the war. It will be my last hurrah."

"Then I will stay with you."

"No, you need to command the flotilla and restrict the Ottoman's ability to reinforce their fortresses."

"Be careful, my friend. I don't want to have to tell your children you died in a conflict they know nothing about."

Paul smiled reassuringly, "Do not have any fears on that front, I will stay safely behind the lines."

Marty didn't want to call him out on what was a blatant untruth. Paul was no more capable of staying out of a fight than he was.

War was declared on March the seventeenth and two thousand Greeks under Mavromichalis marched on Kalamata where they linked up Kolokotronis's army. Nikitaras and Papaflessas commanded divisions.

Kalavryta was put under siege on the twenty-first and the citizens of Patras revolted. The Ottomans counter attacked, but were repelled. By the end of the month the Greeks controlled the countryside and the Turks were confined to their fortresses at Patras, Rio, Acrocorinth, Monemvasia, Nafplion and Tripolitsa. The Greek irregulars besieged them from the landward side but as they had no artillery to speak of they had little chance of stopping them being resupplied from the sea.

The coast of Greece was long and there were many fortresses held by the Turks who, even without the ships the flotilla had burnt, could resupply with little opposition. Marty remembered his promise to the Cretians and sailed down to Heraklion where they joined the Greek fleet. Marty had them sail over the horizon while he sailed the flotilla provocatively close to the harbour.

Chapter 23: Heraklion

Sergeant Major Bright, Anthony or Tony to his friends, watched the long column of revolutionaries move along the road up into the mountains. At every village and junction their numbers grew as men and boys joined. He had only a squad of marines with him having ordered the rest to stay in Pergos. This was not their fight. He was, however, the only one available with any command experience so sat on a horse next to Bishop Dimitris in his black robe and hat.

"We should send out forward scouts and patrols to prevent any Turkish patrols from warning the city," Bright said.

"The mountain men are already clearing the way for us. No Turk or Turkish sympathiser will be alive between here and Heraklion," the bishop replied grimly.

Bright didn't doubt that. They hadn't needed to train the mountain men to fight, only in tactics. They were natural guerrilla fighters, and most were crack shots with their long-barrelled muskets. They were to a man devils with a knife.

They wound their way up the mountain road to the village they stopped at before. This time it took them all day to do the same distance they had done in a morning before. That was one of the joys of marching with a lot of men.

They gathered all the clan chiefs together that evening in the taverna.

"We will surround Heraklion tomorrow," the bishop said. "We will block all the roads to it and prevent any supplies getting into the city by land. The Christians inside will revolt when they see we are in position in two days. If all goes to plan, they will open the gate and let us in."

"Won't the Turks be getting supplies from the sea?" a chieftain asked.

"The Greek Navy and the ships that brought Sergeant Bright and his men will be blockading the port and stopping them from getting supplies or reinforcements."

"What about the other fortresses?" another asked.

"They will be put under siege tomorrow as well. We have men coming in from many of the other islands including Rhodes. They have been deployed to the other fortresses to reinforce our own men."

"What we don't want to do is throw away men storming the walls," Bright said. "We need to get the defenders' attention so the revolt inside can catch them unawares."

"You think we are women?" a particularly belligerent mountain chieftain called.

"I think you are extremely brave men. But to waste your lives would be a sin," Bright responded and the bishop agreed.

There followed a round of who would be where which resulted in several reshuffles as long-standing feuds weren't forgotten. But at midnight they all went to bed knowing what they had to do, come the morning.

The column set out again at dawn. At least the front of it did. The first group to hit the road was the one who would lay siege to the gate. They were followed by the clan responsible for the length of the wall from the gate to the coast. The third group would circle the town and set up from the coast inland to seal off another small gate in the western wall. And so it went with each chieftain's men joining in turn.

Bright joined the first group of a hundred plus men who would seal the road to the gate. The big guns on the walls could reach out two thousand yards so they would start at that range and then move in close enough to be under the guns' minimum elevation. He had a dozen mortars and two hundred bombs he could deploy once they were in range.

They formed up two thousand yards from the walls. A long line of men, weapons glinting in the sunlight. Light reflected from a lens on the wall. Moments later a troop of cavalry came around the fort protecting the gate.

"Form square," Bright advised Dimitris as they had time and didn't want to set stakes yet.

The bishop gave the order and the men did a half-decent job of the evolution, forming the square across the road. The Turks formed into a line and advanced. The square bristled spear points from the inner rank and the front rank raised their muskets to the ready position.

The Turks stopped around a hundred and fifty yards away and looked. The officer rode forward and shouted in bad Greek, "What are you doing?"

Dimitris shouted back, "What does it look like?"

"You are blocking the road."

"We are blocking all the roads. You should surrender."

"Surrender? To a rabble?"

"This is an army not a rabble. The time has come for all Greeks to be free of oppression!"

The last got a roar of approval from the men.

The officer retreated to his men, riding past them towards the city. The troop followed him.

"What will happen now?" Dimitris said.

"He will report to his superiors, and they will decide what to do next. Get the men back into line. They are likely to try their guns next."

Ten minutes later puffs of smoke erupted from the walls. The first volley landed two hundred yards in front of them. Some balls bounced towards them, and one unfortunate was felled.

Their powder is poor quality, Bright realised as he saw the sickly yellow colour of the smoke. *Too much sulphur.* He took a small telescope from his pocket and scanned the terrain between them and the city. It undulated and varied between fields and rough ground. He spotted what he was looking for.

"As soon as it gets dark, we can move the men up to that dry riverbed. They will be sheltered by the bank and inside the guns' minimum range. We can set up the mortars there, and hit the top of the wall."

"The people should be preparing," Dimitris said and was interrupted from any more comments by the blowing of trumpets.

"I believe that the Turks are going to try clearing us away." Bright smiled and pulled his rifle from its saddle sheath.

The guns fired again, and the men fell flat as the balls bounced over their position. The Turks sallied from the fort protecting the gate with cavalry and infantry.

"Prepare the mortars! Set for five-hundred-yards range. Form two ranks."

The brigades on their flanks snuck forward to form a cup-shaped formation with Dimitris' brigade at the base. Bright was pleased. Their training was paying off. More balls came bouncing in and the odd man fell but the men held.

The Turks advanced under the cover of their guns. Janissaries in the middle with other infantry either side and cavalry on their right flank. They looked a picture with their colourful uniforms and flags. Trumpeters and drummers set the pace with what sounded to Bright, a cacophonous noise.

When the Turks got to around five hundred yards Bright said, "They will try and break our lines with the cavalry and follow up with the infantry. Order the mortars to fire."

The mortars started to cough, the deadly black bombs arching forward, smoke trailing from the fuses. They exploded twenty feet above the ground throwing out sheets of razor-sharp iron shards. Almost immediately more bombs followed. Men screamed as they were struck and wounded. The cannons on the wall went quiet and the cavalry charged.

"Forward rank present!"

They got to two hundred yards and Bright and his squad of marines fired their rifles. At eighty yards: "Front rank fire!" The rank blossomed smoke and fire. The brigades on the flanks poured in fire as well.

The effect was mixed; men and horses fell but they still came on and behind them ran the infantry.

"Second rank fire!"

At fifty yards the effect was greater, and a lot of men and horses fell. Still they came and were confronted with a row of spears as the first rank swapped them for their guns. Their horses shied at the hedge of sharp points. The mortars kept firing, shortening their range to target the infantry. The Turks realised they had run into a trap, and that it was turning into a massacre as they took fire from three sides. They broke and ran back to the shelter of the walls.

That night as soon as darkness fell the line moved forward to the riverbed leaving the putrefying corpses of the dead Turks behind them, after looting them of course. Furious digging created a berm along the forward bank of the river behind which they could set up shelters and light cooking fires for a late meal.

"You know the disadvantage of having guns that big on the walls on naval carriages?" Bright asked Corporal Chalmers.

"What's that, Sarge?"

"They can't depress them enough to hit us here."

"Smart to move here then."

"I'm not smart, the commodore worked it out. He is sharper than a razor"

Chalmers laughed; he was used to his sergeant's dry humour.

At daybreak they started to rain a steady stream of bombs onto the top of the wall and the bastions ahead of them. Not too fast so as to conserve ammunition but enough to keep the Turks busy.

There was a roar of guns from the seaward side of the city an hour after dawn.

"That should be the flotilla announcing their blockade," Bright said and sent a man to see what was happening.

Marty and Wolfgang watched the outline of the fort and town resolve itself as the sun rose. The flotilla was a mile offshore at quarters, guns run out. Marty took a big glass and climbed the mizzen ratlines, made himself comfortable on a yard and scanned the city. It was devoid of the usual early morning activities and large numbers of troops were moving from the fort into the city. Puffs of smoke appeared inland, probably over the inland wall.

"Give them their morning wake-up call!" Marty called down.

The guns roared as the entire squadron fired in unison. The noise was incredible, and the air shimmered with the shockwaves from the barrels. The morning breeze blew the smoke towards the city, so it was a few moments before they could see the effect.

The Unicorn's eighteens made the most impact, followed by the Neaera's twelves. The Eagle and Endellion's carronades made a lot of noise. Several chunks were knocked out of the wall of the fort and it had the desired effect as within minutes they could see men manning the guns on the walls and men running back from the town along the causeway.

"Let them have another, then move us out to three miles," Marty said as he regained the deck. That was just beyond the maximum range of the fort's guns. The guns roared again, and Wolfgang ordered the backed foresails to be reset.

"Now we wait to see if their fleet takes the bait."

Much to the men's amusement the officers were dressed as Greeks and the Greek flag flew from the mast. It was all part of the fiction that they were Greek Navy. The idea was that the Turks would take it as a matter of pride, if not necessity, to chase them off. The Greek fleet of ten ships was actually just over the horizon and the flotilla was there to draw the Turkish ships out where they could ambush them.

"Deck there, no activity in the harbour."

"It will probably take them time to respond," Wolfgang mused.

Marty smiled at the sight of the tall, lean Bavarian, dressed in traditional clothes. The trousers were too short for his long legs and the jacket a mite too small as well.

They tacked back and forth giving the crews a taste of what it must have been like to blockade one of the French ports during the war.

"Sail Ho!"

"Where away?"

To the northwest. Coming in fast." There was a pause. "Xebec, Turkish colours."

The ship had the wind gauge on them, but Marty wanted it stopped. Not the least because it must have seen the Greek fleet.

"Signal the schooners to intercept."

The signal flew up the mast and the Eagle and Endellion peeled off in unison setting full sail.

"Deck there, movement in the harbour."

"Of course," Marty said. They would choose to come out when he was two ships down.

It took two hours for the schooners to intercept the onrushing xebec and they were soon engaged in a hot battle that crept ever closer to the flotilla which Marty positioned to intercept them. In the meantime, the ships in the harbour had shaken off their harbour gaskets and were working their way out against the prevailing wind.

"It will be another hour before they get close enough to engage at range," Gordon McGivern said.

"We will edge out to sea. Let them close but slowly I want that xebec taken care of first."

There was a good reason for that. The Endellion was to relay the signal to the Greeks when the flotilla engaged the Turks. The schooners had the xebec bracketed and were pounding her.

"The xebec's mast 'as gone over!" the lookout called.

The Endellion broke off the fight and started for a point somewhere halfway between the Unicorn and the Greek ships.

"Well done, Philip," Wolfgang cheered.

Marty agreed but wished he had the Leonidas and Nymphe with him to make up the numbers.

The seventy-four-gun Sayyad-i bahri was having a hard time getting out of the harbour. Her consorts were clustered around her.

"Admiral, should we let the frigates go ahead and engage them?" Captain Omar Salic said.

"If we had all our ships, yes but without the corvette and two of the xebecs, I will not expose the flagship to unnecessary risk."

The two xebecs and the corvette in question were short of crew. Influenza had ripped through the ships and killed many crewmen a month ago and they had consolidated the men they had left into the ships that had sailed.

The captain fumed silently. The two Greek ships would have had their hands full with the two frigates without the support of the schooners that had gone off to intercept a ship further out. Now they were being drawn ever further from the protection of the fort's guns. In his estimation they would be in range in an hour and by then would be four miles offshore.

Marty watched the Eagle re-join the line just in time as the battle was about to start.

"Hoist the signal for the Greeks to join in," Marty said. Then turned to Wolfgang. "Enough cat and mouse, let's take them on. We have the weather gauge, so use it to keep away from that beast's broadside."

Wolfgang had briefed the flotilla in advance on tactics. They were to harry the Turks and not get into a pounding match which they couldn't win. The agile schooners were to nip at the big ship's heals and try and rake her while the Unicorn and Neaera went for the frigates and xebecs.

The admiral watched the flotilla coming at speed. The schooner that had swung out to the north was now arcing back and being joined by her sister ship. The ship that looked like a converted frigate and the brigantine behind her was looking like they would run down his starboard side. He had a frigate and a xebec out there to shield him. To get at the Sayyad-i bahri they would have to sail between her and her screen and then she would blow them out of the water.

Captain Salic had more sea combat experience than his admiral who had been a soldier in the past and had gotten his post through his family. He considered that the enemy had limited options unless they were to do something suicidal, but that also meant they would never fully engage and defeat them if they kept this formation.

"Admiral, if I may make a suggestion?"

"No."

That settles that then.

The Unicorn bore down on the Turkish fleet. Wolfgang planned to make a close fast pass on the frigate and xebec.

"Ready, all guns!"

The covers on the carronades were removed and the guns swung into line to support the starboard battery. They were also loaded with grape over ball. The main battery was double shotted.

On the Neaera, James and Angus had their twelves double shotted as well. The crews on both ships would have to work fast to get broadsides in on both the frigate and xebec. The Unicorn came up to the frigate's bow and her forward carronades spoke, closely followed by the first eighteen. The frigate shuddered as ball after ball smashed into her bow. The tactic was clear: smash her bow and send her to the bottom.

By the time the Neaera came up, her bow was a mess, her bowsprit was gone as was her figurehead.

"Aim low!" James shouted and the gunners adjusted the angle of the guns. "Fire as you bear! Take her bottom out."

The gunners knew their business and ignored any shot that flew over or past them instead concentrating on firing the moment their barrels came into line with the frigate's bow. The already large hole got bigger and lower. The Unicorn's afterdeck carronades had targeted the frigate's aft and quarterdecks leaving them strewn with bodies.

The admiral watched in astonishment as the enemy ships didn't slow beyond taking a couple of reefs in their mainsails to get them out of the way. He saw the frigate's bow disintegrate as shot after shot was aimed, yes aimed, at it.

"How can they be so accurate?" he said.

"I have heard the British and Americans train their men to aim their guns," Salic said. "Maybe they have been training the Greeks."

The frigate was out of the fight by the time the second ship had passed. Her bow was so badly damaged that she couldn't manoeuvre. She let go of her wind and slowed to a stop. A shout from a lookout brought their attention aft. The schooners were bearing down on their stern! The admiral gawped at them. What were those little ships going to do against his mighty ship.

Trevor Archer had the stern of the seventy-four firmly in his sights. He had steered an arc that would take the two schooners in line astern across its stern, as close as he could manage. That meant crossing behind the Neaera as soon as she cleared the xebec.

Timing would be everything and he had his sail trimmers on standby. *Don't slow down, Angus!*

Angus and James were busy as were their gun crews. They reloaded with chain to target the xebec's rigging. They had no chance to target her bow as the xebec was too close behind the frigate. They fired their broadside and James looked around as they cleared the xebec's stern.

"Bloody hell! Trevor's cutting it close!" he shouted to Angus.

Angus spun to see what James was on about and saw the Eagle almost brush his stern. Trevor raised his hat in salute from his quarterdeck as he passed. Angus laughed and raised his hat in reply.

The stern of the seventy-four was approaching fast and in consideration of his gunners, Trevor ordered them to slow to a more sedate eight knots after they passed the Neaera. His starboard guns were run out. His eight twenty-four-pound carronades loaded with smashers.

"As you bear, shoot him up the arse!"

The carronades fired one by one in a beautiful rolling broadside. The transom windows of the Sayyad-i bahri were stove in and mayhem served on her lower gun deck.

Behind the Eagle, the Endellion was just as ready. Philip Trenchard also saluted the Neaera as they passed a cable behind the Eagle. Her guns added to the death and destruction.

Marty looked at the Turks as they wore to reverse course. They had stung the seventy-four but had by no means hurt it badly. The frigate was dead in the water, her crew frantically trying to wrap a sail around what was left of her bow. Her pumps going continuously. The xebec was hurt, her rigging damaged but still able to fight.

The Greeks were approaching from the north, their sails clearly visible as they rushed to engage their hated enemy.

"Another fifteen minutes before they arrive," Wolfgang said.

"They are turning. Damn they are running for the harbour," Marty exclaimed.

It was true the admiral had seen the approaching fleet and was not prepared to fight all of them. He piled on sail and turned towards the castle. If he could get within their protection he would turn and fight.

Marty swore, they were halfway through wearing and in totally the wrong place to cut them off. The schooners were close but nowhere near powerful enough to make them change direction. It looked like all was lost.

"Deck, there's two ships coming from the northeast. Full sail."

"What? They must be Turks," Gordon said.

"Deck, they are flying the Turkish flag, but I swear it's the Leonidas!"

On the Sayyad-i bahri the admiral was also aware of the oncoming ships. No ships were due from Smyrna, but it could be a patrol. Whatever it was he was thanking God for their intervention.

They would join him before the Greeks caught him. Then he would show them. He ordered a signal raised for them to fall in on the flagship. It was not until they were almost on them when he saw their guns run out and the flag change to the Greek one. They cut across his bow and chain howled through the rigging from bow to stern. Rigging, blocks, spars all fell. The strange ships didn't stop but carried on, joining with a third that was west of them.

Marty crowed with laughter as the Leonidas and Nymphe took down most of the seventy-four's foreword rigging. He had seen James Campbell on the quarterdeck as they passed dressed in full Greek regalia. They had succeeded in slowing the seventy-four but she would still make the edge of the cover of the castle guns. But that didn't put off the Greeks who arrived and swarmed the Turkish fleet.

Onshore Bright heard the guns and after an hour they suddenly saw people on the walls.

"Cease fire."

Bodies fell from the walls and the sound of fighting drifted to them.

"They've revolted a day early," Dimitrius said. "It must have been triggered by the sea battle."

"Get the men ready."

Chapter 24: Paul's Last Battle

Paul started out with the best intentions of keeping his word to Marty. However, as they approached Phocis he couldn't resist moving up to the front. He joined the army of Anthanasios Diakos, a thirty-year-old, classically handsome man with flowing dark hair and moustache. He was an ordained Deacon of the Greek orthodox church. He was now a leader of the resistance and a leading member of the Filiki Eteria.

They marched to Livadeia. The battle was intense, but they had caught the Turks by surprise and the victory was never in doubt. It was followed by the capture of Thebes two days later. Everything was going swimmingly.

That was until the Turks put Albanian General Omer Vrioni, in command of their forces in the Roumeli, with eight thousand Albanians under his command.

Diakos made a stand at the river Alamana near Thermopylae with an additional fifteen hundred men commanded by Panourgias and Dyovouniotis.

"What do you know about this Ottoman general?" Paul asked.

"He is an Albanian and is an animal. He has no honour and hates Greeks. He kills them for sport," Diakos replied.

"Is he experienced?"

"He has fought many battles."

The Greek force of fifteen hundred men was split into three sections. Dyovouniotis was to defend the bridge at Gorgoptamos, Panourgias, the heights of Halkomata, and Diakos, the bridge at Alamana. It was a strong defensive position and Diakos was confident that their fifteen hundred could stop the eight thousand. However, they had the mountains at their back and Paul wondered why they didn't choose somewhere there to make a stand. Then it occurred to him that the proximity of this battlefield to Thermopolyia must be a major influence.

"I need to get to high ground," Paul said. There was a hill off to the right which was anchoring their right flank. He took a horse and rode up it at a canter. Once at the top, he had a panoramic view of the battlefield.

"Oh Shit!" he said.

Vrioni had split his force into two. Initially it wasn't clear what his intention was. Their artillery was set back but well in range of the Greek positions and was trained on the Greek centre. Puffs of smoke from the cannon were a prelude to the Albanian advance. One force was heading for Diakos the other turned and headed for the bridge,

The Ottomans advanced as he spurred his horse down the slope, he was halfway down when the horse stumbled in a burrow and broke its leg. Paul was thrown over the doomed animal's head. He just had time to tuck in his shoulder and land in a roll. The horse lay on the ground screaming in pain. Paul didn't hesitate but drew a pistol and put it out of its misery.

He was winded and had to stand for a minute to fully regain his breath. *Damn I'm not as fit as I once was.*

Recovered, he set out for the lines, but he could see that he was going to be too late as four thousand men descended on the bridge in a column nine men wide. They marched shoulder to shoulder halberds to the front. All the Greeks could do was shoot their guns and reload as fast as they could. It was hopeless. Every time a man fell another stepped up into his place.

They were unstoppable.

It was a rout.

Then they turned towards Halkomata on the heights. With the same result.

Paul managed to grab a horse that had broken its tether and set out to find Odysseas Androutsos. He caught up with him trying to reform his scattered troops.

"It is hopeless Paul. They were not prepared for such an assault."

"Will Diakos retreat?"

"I do not think so. He is a proud man."

"Then he is foolish as well as proud."

Paul was right, Diakos and his men held out for several hours before being overwhelmed by the Albanians. The severely-wounded Diakos was taken alive. He was offered a position in the Ottoman army, asked to swear fealty to the Sultan and convert to Islam. He refused saying, "I lived a Greek. I shall die a Greek." They threatened to roast him alive. He still refused so they impaled him on a spit and slow-roasted him. Afterwards his death was romanticised and used as a rallying call for Greeks everywhere. The poets claimed that as they took him to be executed, he is said to have sung,

"Oh, what a moment Death chose for me to perish. Spring grass everywhere and branches with blossoms to cherish."

Paul sat at a campfire with Androutsos and two other Greek captains Panourgias and Dyovouniotis.

"We need to stop the Ottomans from getting their men to the Peloponnese," Androutsos said.

"How, we have less than four hundred men between us." Panourgias said and Dyovouniotis agreed. "Dimitri is right. They have eight thousand of those damned Albanians. We cannot stop them. It would be suicide."

"But you can slow them down if you choose the right place to hold them. I did it to the French in Spain," Paul said.

"How?"

"We took over a fortified position that straddled the road in a pass. We held it for a long time and did some real damage to the French with just a small force of partisans and marines. Is there anywhere like that on the road to the south?"

"The Inn at Gravia is a bit like that," Androutsos said. "It is built of stone and sits at the entrance to the pass south. They would have to stop and clear us out or we would cut their supply line."

"You would never hold it. I will not commit my men to a suicide mission. It's better if we disperse into the high ground on either side and do hit and run attacks," Dimitri Panourgias said.

"I want to see it," Paul said. "Then we can decide."

The inn was a short five miles away. Brick-built above a three-foot-high stone foundation the single-storey inn had a row of small windows facing outwards and a walled courtyard.

"It's a trap," Panourgias said, "you will never get away."

"We will, but, more importantly, they will not be able to storm it and that courtyard is a trap for them," Paul said.

"They will just come through the gate. I could knock it down by blowing on it," Dyovouniotis said.

"That's perfect," Paul said with a smile.

"What?"

"If they come through that gate, they will present a front of what six or seven men at a time? If we have three rows of muskets lined up firing rolling volleys—"

"We will decimate them," grinned Androutsos.

In the end after a lot of argument Androutsos and Paul with one hundred and twenty men shut themselves in the farmhouse and the rest dispersed into the hills to provide supporting fire. They set up three ranks of twenty men facing the gate; the rest dispersed throughout the inn.

The Albanian troops advanced after resting up at their camp at Lianokladi. The twelve-mile march to Gravia took them all morning and they surrounded the inn in the early afternoon.

"What are they waiting for?" a soldier asked Paul who had command of the ranks in the courtyard.

"Organising themselves probably. Their commander seems to have a thing for order." Paul smiled reassuringly. "Remember, you fire in ranks and aim low. As soon as you fire you reload and wait for the order to present and fire again. This way the enemy has to face a continuous hail of balls. We will massacre them."

Drums started to beat, and trumpets blew. The sound of hundreds of men advancing rumbled through the air. Paul stood at the end of the first rank calm and relaxed. The men noticed and nerves were settled.

The sound of marching grew louder. The men in the windows started to shoot. There was a crash and the gates burst inwards. A group of startled Albanians with a battering ram stood in the open gate. Paul didn't give the order and let them move to the side allowing the main force to advance.

"First rank, present!" He paused to allow the advancing horde to get to the opening. "FIRE!"

Smoke and flame spouted from the twenty muskets then the men reloaded. Every man in the front two rows fell, either from the bullet hitting him directly or from a bullet passing through the man in front and hitting the man behind.

"Second rank, present. FIRE!" Paul called the volleys and by the time the third rank had fired the first was ready again.

"Steady! First rank, present. FIRE!"

They couldn't see what they were shooting at for smoke. Paul paused and listened. All he could hear were the groans of the wounded. He checked his ranks. One man was wounded, the rest were fine.

The smoke cleared, blown away on a gentle breeze. The gate was piled with dead and wounded soldiers.

"Damn, there must be thirty or more." Paul moved forward to look out of the gate. The Ottomans were reforming. He glanced along the side of the building. There were more dead and dying lying in front of that.

Drums started beating. Trumpets blew. The army advanced again. Paul moved his men up behind the wall of dead using them as a barricade. Apart from that it was the same again.

"Front rank, present. FIRE!"

"Second rank, present. FIRE!"

"Third rank, present. FIRE!"

More men died and it continued until dark when the Albanians withdrew.

"What do you think they will do now?" Odysseas said to Paul.

"If it were me, I would bring up artillery and bombard this place to rubble."

"Then we should leave."

"I totally agree. Let's get the men away and into the hills. We can carry on the fight up there."

Epilogue

The Ottomans brought up their artillery only to find an empty building. Paul and his team had melted away into the hills in the dark. The Ottomans lost three hundred dead and over six hundred wounded in just a couple of hours of fighting. The Greeks only lost six.

Was it worth it? Yes, because Omer Vrioni withdrew to the Island of Euboea and waited for reinforcements. They had managed to instil doubt and uncertainty into his mind and that gave the Greeks time to consolidate their hold on the Peloponnese and Central Greece if only for a short time but that is another story.

The whole flotilla reassembled after the sea battle and to say the least they had a bit of a party before going their separate ways. Afterwards they picked up Paul and went back to the Ionian Islands to pick up Billy. Billy, however, wanted to stay with Veronica and, ever the romantic, Marty let him. He would have to find a new muscle man. They returned to Portugal, leaving the Leonidas and Nymphe to continue patrolling the Aegean, where Caroline and their household boarded the Pride. Marty joined them. It was time to return to England for the coronation. George was expecting them and it didn't do to disappoint one's king.

As was always the way in Greece, it didn't take long for the factions to argue over who was in charge of what. With discord and internal conflict rife, all the Ottomans had to do was wait.

Historical notes

First off, a note to explain why Beth's mission hasn't been included in detail. As I have written more about her, I realised she deserves a series to herself. You can find out how she got on at the academy and in her first missions in The Dorset Boy – Lady Bethany – Graduation.

One pound sterling was the equivalent of one hundred pounds in today's money. On that basis Marty's salary from the navy was around one hundred thousand a year.

Likewise, the coronation cost of £230,000 translates to around £21,000,000.

Any mention of telegraphs is referring to semaphore towers or Optical Telegraphs not Electrical Telegraphs.

Chargé d'affaires are put in place when there is no ambassador in residence, or the ambassador is remote. The position is one rank down from Ambassador.

The city of Smyrna mentioned in this book changed its name to Izmir in 1928. However, the original name is still used in some languages around the world.

The town of Vostitsa is modern Aigion.

The articles of war are often quoted in books as I do here. This set of rules applied to the navy in peace as well as war and was effectively the rulebook for the operation of a ship. To save you having to look them up I have copied these from Wikipedia.

The following articles and orders were established from the 25th of December 1749; and are directed to be observed and put in execution, as well in time of peace as in time of war.[8]

I. Divine worship. All commanders, captains, and officers, in or belonging to any of His Majesty's ships or vessels of war, shall cause the public worship of Almighty God, according to the liturgy of the Church of England established by law, to be solemnly, orderly and reverently performed in their respective ships; and shall take care that prayers and preaching, by the chaplains in holy orders of the respective ships, be performed diligently; and that the Lord's day be observed according to law.

II. Swearing, Drunkenness, scandalous actions, &c. All flag officers, and all persons in or belonging to His Majesty's ships or vessels of war, being guilty of profane oaths, cursings, execrations, drunkenness, uncleanness, or other scandalous actions, in derogation of God's honour, and corruption of good manners, shall incur such punishment as a court martial shall think fit to impose, and as the nature and degree of their offence shall deserve.

III. Holding intelligence with an enemy, or rebel. If any officer, mariner, soldier, or other person of the fleet, shall give, hold, or entertain intelligence to or with any enemy or rebel, without leave from the king's majesty, or the lord high admiral, or the commissioners for executing the office of lord high admiral, commander in chief, or his commanding officer, every such person so offending, and being thereof convicted by the sentence of a court martial, shall be punished with death.

IV. Letter or message from an enemy, or rebel. If any letter of message from any enemy or rebel, be conveyed to any officer, mariner, or soldier or other in the fleet, and the said officer, mariner, or soldier, or other as aforesaid, shall not, within twelve hours, having opportunity so to do, acquaint his superior or a commanding officer, or if any superior officer being acquainted therewith, shall not in convenient time reveal the same to the commander in chief of the squadron, every such person so offending, and being convicted thereof by the sentence of the court martial, shall be punished with death, or such other punishment as the nature and degree of the offence shall deserve, and the court martial shall impose.

V. Spies, and all persons in the nature of spies. All spies, and all persons whatsoever, who shall come, or be found, in the nature of spies, to bring or deliver any seducing letters or messages from any enemy or rebel, or endeavour to corrupt any captain, officer, mariner, or other in the fleet, to betray his trust, being convicted of any such offence by the sentence of the court martial, shall be punished with death, or such other punishment, as the nature and degree of the offence shall deserve, and the court martial shall impose.

VI. Relieving an enemy or rebel. No person in the fleet shall relieve an enemy or rebel with money, victuals, powder, shot, arms, ammunition, or any other supplies whatsoever, directly or indirectly, upon pain of death, or such other punishment as the court martial shall think fit to impose, and as the nature and degree of the crime shall deserve.

VII. Papers, &c. found on board of prizes. All the papers, charter parties, bills of lading, passports, and other writings whatsoever, that shall be taken, seized, or found aboard any ship or ships which shall be surprized or taken as prize, shall be duly preserved, and the very originals shall by the commanding officer of the ship which shall take such prize, be sent entirely, and without fraud, to the court of the admiralty, or such other court of commissioners, as shall be authorized to determine whether such prize be lawful capture, there to be viewed, made use of, and proceeded upon according to law, upon pain that every person offending herein, shall forfeit and lose his share of the capture, and shall suffer such further punishment, as the nature and degree of his offence shall be found to deserve, and the court martial shall impose.

VIII. Taking money or good out of prizes. No person in or belonging to the fleet shall take out of any prize, or ship seized for prize, any money, plate, or goods, unless it shall be necessary for the better securing thereof, or for the necessary use and service of any of His Majesty's ships or vessels of war, before the same be adjudged lawful prize in some admiralty court; but the full and entire account of the whole, without embezzlement, shall be brought in, and judgement passed entirely upon the whole without fraud, upon pain that every person offending herein shall forfeit and lose his share of the capture, and suffer such further punishment as shall be imposed by a court martial, or such court of admiralty, according to the nature and degree of the offence.

IX. Stripping or ill treating prisoners. If any ship or vessel be taken as prize, none of the officers, mariners, or other persons on board her, shall be stripped of their clothes, or in any sort pillaged, beaten, or evil-intreated, upon the pain that the person or persons so offending, shall be liable to such punishment as a court martial shall think fit to inflict.

X. Preparation for fight. Every flag officer, captain and commander in the fleet, who, upon signal or order of fight, or sight of any ship or ships which it may be his duty to engage, or who, upon likelihood of engagement, shall not make the necessary preparations for fight, and shall not in his own person, and according to his place, encourage the inferior officers and men to fight courageously, shall suffer death, or such other punishment, as from the nature and degree of the offence a court martial shall deem him to deserve; and if any person in the fleet shall treacherously or cowardly yield or cry for quarter, every person so offending, and being convicted thereof by the sentence of a court martial, shall suffer death.

XI. Obedience to orders in battle. Every person in the fleet, who shall not duly observe the orders of the admiral, flag officer, commander of any squadron or division, or other his superior officer, for assailing, joining battle with, or making defence against any fleet, squadron, or ship, or shall not obey the orders of his superior officer as aforesaid in the time of action, to the best of his power, or shall not use all possible endeavours to put the same effectually into execution, every person so offending, and being convicted thereof by the sentence of the court martial, shall suffer death, or such other punishment, as from the nature and degree of the offence a court martial shall deem him to deserve.

XII. Withdrawing or keeping back from fight, &c. Every person in the fleet, who through cowardice, negligence, or disaffection, shall in time of action withdraw or keep back, or not come into the fight or engagement, or shall not do his utmost to take or destroy every ship which it shall be his duty to engage, and to assist and relieve all and every of His Majesty's ships, or those of his allies, which it shall be his duty to assist and relieve, every such person so offending, and being convicted thereof by the sentence of a court martial, shall suffer death.

XIII. Forbearing to pursue an enemy, &c. Every person in the fleet, who though cowardice, negligence, or disaffection, shall forbear to pursue the chase of any enemy, pirate or rebel, beaten or flying; or shall not relieve or assist a known friend in view to the utmost of his power; being convicted of any such offence by the sentence of a court martial, shall suffer death.

XIV. Delaying or discouraging any service. If when action, or any service shall be commanded, any person in the fleet shall presume or to delay or discourage the said action or service, upon pretence of arrears of wages, or upon any pretence whatsoever, every person so offending, being convicted thereof by the sentence of the court martial, shall suffer death, or such other punishment, as from the nature and degree of the offence a court martial shall deem him to deserve.

XV. Deserting to an enemy; running away with ships stores. Every person in or belonging to the fleet, who shall desert to the enemy, pirate, or rebel, or run away with any of His Majesty's ships or vessels of war, or any ordnance, ammunition, stores, or provision belonging thereto, to the weakening of the service, or yield up the same cowardly or treacherously to the enemy, pirate, or rebel, being convicted of any such offence by the sentence of the court martial, shall suffer death.

XVI. Desertion, and entertaining deserters. Every person in or belonging to the fleet, who shall desert or entice others so to do, shall suffer death, or such other punishment as the circumstances of the offence shall deserve, and a court martial shall judge fit: and if any commanding officer of any of His Majesty's ships or vessels of war shall receive or entertain a deserter from any other of His Majesty's ships or vessels, after discovering him to be such deserter, and shall not with all convenient speed give notice to the captain of the ship or vessel to which such deserter belongs; or if the said ships or vessels are at any considerable distance from each other, to the secretary of the admiralty, or to the commander in chief; every person so offending, and being convicted thereof by the sentence of the court martial, shall be cashiered.

XVII. Convoys. The officers and seamen of all ships appointed for convoy and guard of merchant ships, or of any other, shall diligently attend upon that charge, without delay, according to their instructions in that behalf; and whosoever shall be faulty therein, and shall not faithfully perform their duty, and defend the ships and goods in their convoy, without either diverting to other parts or occasions, or refusing or neglecting to fight in their defence, if they be assailed, or running away cowardly, and submitting the ships in their convoy to peril and hazard; or shall demand or exact any money or other reward from any merchant or master for convoying any ships or vessels entrusted to their care, or shall misuse the masters or mariners thereof; shall be condemned to make reparation of the damage to the merchants, owners, and others, as the court of admiralty shall adjudge, and also be punished criminally according to the quality of their offences, be it by pains of death, or other punishment, according as shall be adjudged fit by the court martial.

XVIII. Receiving goods and merchandize on board. If any captain commander, or other officer of any of His Majesty's ships or vessels shall receive on board, or permit to be received on board such ship or vessel, any goods or merchandizes whatsoever, other than for the sole use of the ship or vessel, except gold, silver, or jewels, and except the goods and merchandizes belonging to any merchant, or other ship or vessel which may be shipwrecked, or in imminent danger of being shipwrecked, either on the high seas, or in any port creek, or harbour, in order to the preserving them for their proper owners, and except such goods or merchandizes as he shall at any time be ordered to take or receive on board by order of the lord high admiral of Great Britain, or the commissioners for executing the office of lord high admiral for the time being; every person so offending being convicted thereof by the sentence of the court martial shall be cashiered, and be for ever afterwards rendered incapable to serve in any place or office in the naval service of His Majesty, his heirs and successors.

XIX. Mutinous assembly. Uttering words of sedition and mutiny Contempt to superior officers. If any person in or belonging to the fleet shall make or endeavour to make any mutinous assembly upon any pretence whatsoever, every person offending herein, and being convicted thereof by the sentence of the court martial, shall suffer death: and if any person in or belonging to the fleet shall utter any words of sedition or mutiny, he shall suffer death, or such other punishment as a court martial shall deem him to deserve: and if any officer, mariner, or soldier on or belonging to the fleet, shall behave himself with contempt to his superior officer, being in the execution of his office, he shall be punished according to the nature of his offence by the judgement of a court martial.

XX. Concealing traitorous or mutinous designs, &c. If any person in the fleet shall conceal any traitorous or mutinous practice or design, being convicted thereof by the sentence of a court martial, he shall suffer death, or any other punishment as a court martial shall think fit; and if any person, in or belonging to the fleet, shall conceal any traitorous or mutinous words spoken by any, to the prejudice of His Majesty or government, or any words, practice, or design, tending to the hindrance of the service, and shall not forthwith reveal the same to the commanding officer, or being present at any mutiny or sedition, shall not use his utmost endeavours to suppress the same, he shall be punished as a court martial shall think he deserves.

XXI. No person upon any pretence to attempt to stir up disturbance. If any person in the fleet shall find cause of complaint of the unwholesomeness of the victual, or upon other just ground, he shall quietly make the same known to his superior, or captain, or commander in chief, as the occasion may deserve, that such present remedy may be had as the matter may require; and the said superior, captain, or commander in chief, shall, as far as he is able, cause the same to be presently remedied; and no person in the fleet, upon any such or other pretence, shall attempt to stir up any disturbance, upon pain of such punishment, as a court martial shall think fit to inflict, according to the degree of the offence.

XXII. Striking a superior officer. Quarelling. Disobedience. If any officer, mariner, soldier or other person in the fleet, shall strike any of his superior officers, or draw, or offer to draw, or lift up any weapon against him, being in the execution of his office, on any pretence whatsoever, every such person being convicted of any such offence, by the sentence of a court martial, shall suffer death; and if any officer, mariner, soldier or other person in the fleet, shall presume to quarrel with any of his superior officers, being in the execution of his office, or shall disobey any lawful command of any of his superior officers; every such person being convicted of any such offence, by the sentence of a court martial, shall suffer death, or such other punishment, as shall, according to the nature and degree of his offence, be inflicted upon him by the sentence of a court martial.

XXIII. Fighting. Provoking speeches, &c. If any person in the fleet shall quarrel or fight with any other person in the fleet, or use reproachful or provoking speeches or gestures, tending to make any quarrel or disturbance, he shall, upon being convicted thereof, suffer such punishment as the offence shall deserve, and a court martial shall impose.

XXIV. Embezzlement of stores. There shall be no wasteful expence of any powder, shot, ammunition, or other stores in the fleet, nor any embezzlement thereof, but the stores and provisions shall be careful preserved, upon pain of such punishment to be inflicted upon the offenders, abettors, buyers and receivers (being persons subject to naval discipline) as shall be by a court martial found just in that behalf.

XXV. Burning a magazine, ship, &c. Every person in the fleet, who shall unlawfully burn or set fire to any magazine or store of powder, or ship, boat, ketch, hoy or vessel, or tackle or furniture thereunto belonging, not then appertaining to an enemy, pirate, or rebel, being convicted of any such offence, by the sentence of a court martial, shall suffer death.

XXVI. Steering and conducting ships, &c. Care shall be taken in the conducting and steering of any of His Majesty's ships, that through wilfulness, negligence, or other defaults, no ship be stranded, or run upon any rocks or sands, or split or hazarded, upon pain, that such as shall be found guilty therein, be punished by death, or such other punishment, as the offence by a court martial shall be judged to deserve.

XXVII. Sleeping, negligence, and forsaking a station. No person in or belonging to the fleet shall sleep upon his watch, or negligently perform the duty imposed on him, or forsake his station, upon pain of death, or such other punishment as a court martial shall think fit to impose, and as the circumstances of the case shall require.

XXVIII. Murder. All murders committed by any person in the fleet, shall be punished with death by the sentence of a court martial.

XXIX. Sodomy. If any person in the fleet shall commit the unnatural and detestable sin of buggery and sodomy with man or beast, he shall be punished with death by the sentence of a court martial.

XXX. Robbery. All robbery committed by any person in the fleet, shall be punished with death, or otherwise, as a court martial, upon consideration of the circumstances, shall find meet.

XXXI. False musters. Every officer or other person in the fleet, who shall knowingly make or sign a false muster or muster book, or who shall command, counsel, or procure the making or signing thereof, or who shall aid or abet any other person in the making or signing thereof, shall, upon proof of any such offence being made before a court martial, be cashiered, and rendered incapable of further employment in His Majesty's naval service.

XXXII. Apprehending and keeping criminals. Bringing offenders to punishment. No provost martial belonging to the fleet shall refuse to apprehend any criminal, whom he shall be authorized by legal warrant to apprehend, or to receive or keep any prisoner committed to his charge, or wilfully suffer him to escape, being once in his custody, or dismiss him without lawful order, upon pain of such punishment as a court martial shall deem him fit to deserve; and all captains, officers, and others in the fleet, shall do their endeavour to detect, apprehend, and bring to punishment all offenders, and shall assist the officers appointed for that purpose therein, upon pain of being proceeded against, and punished by a court martial, according to the nature and degree of the offence.

XXXIII. Behaving unbecoming an officer. If any flag officer, captain, or commander, or lieutenant belonging to the fleet, shall be convicted before a court martial of behaving in a scandalous, infamous, cruel, oppressive, or fraudulent manner, unbecoming the character of an officer, he shall be dismissed from His Majesty's service.

XXXIV. Mutiny, desertion, disobedience when on shore, in the king's dominions. Every person being in actual service and full pay, and part of the crew in or belonging to any of His Majesty's ships or vessels of war, who shall be guilty of mutiny, desertion, or disobedience to any lawful command, in any part of His Majesty's dominions on shore, when in actual service relative to the fleet, shall be liable to be tried by a court martial, and suffer the like punishment for every such offence, as if the same had been committed at sea on board any of His Majesty's ships or vessels of war.

XXXV. Crimes committed on shore out of the king's dominions. If any person who shall be in the actual service and full pay of His Majesty's ships and vessels of war, shall commit upon the shore, in any place or places out of His Majesty's dominions, any of the crimes punishable by these articles and orders, the person so offending shall be liable to be tried and punished for the same, in like manner, to all intents and purposes, as if the same crimes had been committed at sea, on board any of His Majesty's ships or vessels of war.

XXXVI. Crimes not mentioned in this act. All other crimes not capital committed by any person or persons in the fleet, which are not mentioned in this act, or for which no punishment is hereby directed to be inflicted, shall be punished by the laws and customs in such cases used at sea.

Glossary of sailing terms used in this book

Beam – The **beam** of a ship is its width at its widest point

Bowsprit – a spar projecting from the bow of a vessel, especially a sailing vessel, used to carry the headstay as far forward as possible.

Cable – A cable length or length of cable is a nautical unit of measure equal to one tenth of a nautical mile or approximately 100 fathoms. Owing to anachronisms and varying techniques of measurement, a cable length can be anywhere from 169 to 220 metres, depending on the standard used. In this book we assume 200 yards.

Cay – a low bank or reef of coral, rock, or sand especially one on the islands in Spanish America.

Futtock shrouds – are rope, wire or chain links in the rigging of a traditional square-rigged ship. They run from the outer edges of a top downwards and inwards to a point on the mast or lower shrouds, and carry the load of the shrouds that rise from the edge of the top. This prevents any tendency of the top itself to tilt relative to the mast.

Gripe – to tend to come up into the wind in spite of the helm.

Ketch – a two-masted sailing vessel, fore-and-aft rigged with a tall mainmast and a mizzen stepped forward of the rudderpost.

Knee – is a natural or cut, curved piece of wood.[1] Knees, sometimes called ships knees, are a common form of bracing in boatbuilding.

Knot – the measure of speed at sea. 1 knot = 1.11 miles.

Leeway – the leeward drift of a ship i.e. with the wind towards the lee side.

Loblolly boys – Surgeon's assistants

Lugger – a sailing vessel defined by its rig using the lug sail on all of its one or several masts. They were widely used as working craft, particularly off the coast. Luggers varied extensively in size and design. Many were undecked, open boats. Others were fully decked.

Mizzen – 1. on a yawl, ketch or dandy the after mast.

> **2.** (on a vessel with three or more masts) the third mast from the bow.

Pawls – a catch that drops into the teeth of a capstan to stop it being pulled in reverse.

In ordinary – vessels "in ordinary" (from the 17th century) are those out of service for repair or maintenance, a meaning coming over time to cover a reserve fleet or "mothballed" ships.

Ratlines – are lengths of thin line tied between the shrouds of a sailing ship to form a ladder. Found on all square-rigged ships, whose crews must go aloft to stow the square sails, they also appear on larger fore-and-aft rigged vessels to aid in repairs aloft or conduct a lookout from above.

Rib – a thin strip of pliable timber laid athwarts inside a hull from inwale to inwale at regular close intervals to reinforce its planking. Ribs differ from frames or futtocks in being far smaller dimensions and bent in place compared to frames or futtocks, which are normally sawn to shape, or natural crooks that are shaped to fit with an adze, axe or chisel.

Sea anchor – any device, such as a bucket or canvas funnel, dragged in the water to keep a vessel heading into the wind or reduce drifting.

Shrouds – on a sailing boat, the shrouds are pieces of standing rigging which hold the mast up from side to side. There is frequently more than one shroud on each side of the boat. Usually, a shroud will connect at the top of the mast, and additional shrouds might connect partway down the mast, depending on the design of the boat. Shrouds terminate at their bottom ends at the chain plates, which are tied into the hull. They are sometimes held outboard by channels, a ledge that keeps the shrouds clear of the gunwales.

Stay – is part of the standing RIGGING and is used to support the weight of a mast. It is a large strong rope extending from the upper end of each mast.

Sweeps – another name for oars.

Tack – if a sailing ship is tacking or if the people in it tack it, it is sailing towards a particular point in a series of lateral movements rather than in a direct line.

Tumblehome – a hull which grows narrower above the waterline than its beam.

Wear ship – to change the tack of a sailing vessel, especially a square-rigger, by coming about so that the wind passes astern.

Weather Gauge – sometimes spelled weather gage is the advantageous position of a fighting sailing vessel relative to another. It is also known as "nautical gauge" as it is related to the sea shore.

If you have any questions, complaints or suggestions:
Please visit my website: www.thedorsetboy.com where you can leave a message or subscribe to the newsletter.

Or like and follow my Facebook page:

Or I can be found on twitter @ChristoperCTu3

Books by Christopher C Tubbs

The Dorset Boy Series.
A Talent for Trouble
The Special Operations Flotilla
Agent Provocateur
In Dangerous Company
The Tempest
Vendetta
The Trojan Horse
La Licorne
Raider
Silverthorn
Exile
Dynasty
Empire
Revolution

The Scarlet Fox Series
Scarlett
A Kind of Freedom
Legacy

The Charlamagne Griffon Chronicles
Buddha's Fist
The Pharoah's Mask
Treasure of the Serpent God
The Knights Templar

See them all at:

Website: www.thedorsetboy.com
Twitter: @ChristoherCTu3
Facebook: https://www.facebook.com/thedorsetboy/
YouTube: https://youtu.be/KCBR4ITqDi4

Published in E-Book, Paperback and Audio formats on Amazon, Audible and iTunes

Printed in Great Britain
by Amazon